2024

Training

mit Original-Prüfungen

Integrierte Gesamtschule
Niedersachsen

Englisch 10. Klasse

STARK

Bildnachweis

Deckblätter
S. 1 Deckblatt „Übungsaufgaben zu den Kompetenzbereichen" © Willselarep|Dreamstime.com
S. 93 Deckblatt „Original-Prüfungsaufgaben" © wavebreakmedia. Shutterstock

Listening
S. 5 Uhrzeiten © moviephoto/shutterstock
S. 7 Taxis New York © Tono Balaguer. 123rf.com; Känguru © Christopher Meder. Shutterstock; Safari © luisapuccini. 123rf.com; Kreditkarte © wavebreakmedia ltd. Shutterstock; Münzen © Oliver Hoffmann. Shutterstock; 5-Pfund-Schein © Can Stock Photo/aaronamat; Digitalziffern © DVARG. Shutterstock
S. 8 Eis mit Kirsche © karen roach. Shutterstock; Fish and Chips © Janet Faye Hastings. Shutterstock; Block Papier © peshkova.123rf.com; Buchcover © foxie. Shutterstock; Farbtöpfe © Petrenko Andriy. Shutterstock; T-Shirt © Tarzhanova. Shutterstock; Pullover © indigo-fotos. Shutterstock; Filzstifte © Ruslan Kerimov. Shutterstock; Buntstifte © kamomeen. Shutterstock; schwarze Katze von der Seite (links und rechts) © Eric Isselee. Shutterstock; Katze von hinten © Can Stock Photo/Ivonne Wierink
S. 9 Business Class © Richair|Dreamstime.com; Economy Class (1B/C) © Aleksandr Kurganov|Dreamstime.com; Taxi © Roland Nagy|Dreamstime.com; Bus © Tupungato|Dreamstime.com; Zug © Johnscoolphotos/shutterstock; Illustration „Marketplace" © Paul Jenkinson; London © QQ7. Shutterstock; Strand © MartiniDry. Shutterstock; Park © Peter Radacsi/shutterstock
S. 10 Flughafen © Rob Wilson. Shutterstock; Café © Kevin George|Dreamstime.com; Wohnzimmer © Ambient Ideas. Shutterstock; Taxis © Innershadows|Dreamstime.com; Frühstücksbüffet © Supparsorn Wantarnagon|Dreamstime.com; Bänke © Tupungato | Dreamstime.com
S. 11 Hai © Eric Isselée. Fotolia.com; Goldnugget © Steffen Foerster. Shutterstock
S. 12 Bild „California Gold Rush" © 2733991. Shutterstock
S. 14 Müll am Strand © Fabien Monteil. Shutterstock; Edinburgh Castle © jan kranendonk. Shutterstock
S. 15 Kind © Nikol Senkyrikova|Dreamstime

Reading
S. 20 Mountainbike © 123rf.com; Feuerstelle © Valery Ivashchenko|Dreamstime.com; Flugzeug © WojciechBeczynski. Shutterstock; Handtasche © Zaclurs|Dreamstime.com
S. 24 Lilly © Andresr. Shutterstock; Kathy © ostill. Shutterstock; Simon © 123rf.com; Gemma © Dean Drobot/shutterstock; Charlie © michaeljung. Shutterstock
S. 28 Dachgarten © Alisonh29/Dreamstime.com

Mediating
S. 34 Schild c © Amy Van Winkle. 123rf.com
S. 35 Schild d – Illustration gebrochenes Eis © seamartini. 123rf.com; Schild e © Robert J. Beyers II. Shutterstock; Schild f © Ricky Corey. 123rf.com
S. 36 Schild e (Hintergrund) © Harun Ozmen/shutterstock
S. 37 Poster „Autumn Festival" © Vector Tradition SM. Fotolia.com
S. 38 afrikanisches Dorf © Paul Jenkinson
S. 42 Sonne © LEWEB. Shutterstock
S. 44 Fenster © Jürgen Fälche – Fotolia.de; München © Stefan Kühn, lizensiert unter CC BY-SA 3.0; Mädchen beim Schaukeln © Pavel Lysenko – Fotolia.de; Restaurant © Sebastian Czapnik|Dreamstime.com
S. 45 Quadfahren im Schlamm © Can Stock Photo/BrandonSeidel; Quadfahren am Strand © Can Stock Photo/james74

Writing
S. 57 Regenschirm © 123rf.com; Frau mit Gitarre © spaxiax. Shutterstock
S. 58 Briefumschlag mit E-Mail-Symbol © Can Stock Photo Inc./vasabii
S. 59 Schulmotive © yunna gorskaya. 123rf.com
S. 60 griechische Insel © Kwiatek7. Shutterstock
S. 61 Bügeleisen © Neveshkin Nikolay. Shutterstock; Hemd © belchonock. 123rf.com
S. 62 London © boybehindacamera/shutterstock
S. 64 Junge nach Mobbingvorfall © mandy godbehear|123RF
S. 65 Golden Gate Bridge © Jay Beiler|Dreamstime.com; Cable Car © Minyun Zhou|Dreamstime.com
S. 67 Mädchen mit Smartphone © Syda Productions|Dreamstime.com
S. 68 Frau © PathDoc. Shutterstock; Baustelle © Devin_Pavel. Shutterstock; Hotelzimmer © Dreamshot|Dreamstime.com; Kakerlake © 607708. Shutterstock

Speaking
S. 77 Mädchen im Gespräch © Jan Martin Will|Dreamstime.com
S. 80 Mädchen vor Computer © Monkey Business Images Ltd.|Dreamstime.com; Kinder im Klassenzimmer © Dawn Shearer Simonetti. Shutterstock
S. 81 Notizzettel © amasterphotographer. Shutterstock; Mädchen im Klassenzimmer © Emil Kudahl Christensen|Dreamstime.com; World AIDS Day © Allies Interactive Services Private Limited|Dreamstime.com; Holzzug © Ntcandrej|Dreamstime.com; Hund © Susan Schmitz. Shutterstock; Umweltschützer*innen © Wavebreakmedia Ltd|Dreamstime.com

4. ergänzte Auflage
www.stark-verlag.de

Inhalt

Sobald die Original-Prüfungsaufgaben 2023 freigegeben sind, können sie als PDF auf der Plattform MyStark heruntergeladen werden (Zugangscode vgl. Umschlaginnenseite).

Autorinnen und Autoren

Listening: Paul Jenkinson, Redaktion
Reading: Paul Jenkinson, Redaktion
Mediating: Heike Burfeind, Paul Jenkinson, Redaktion
Writing: Heike Burfeind, Paul Jenkinson, Redaktion
Speaking: Birte Bendrich, Paul Jenkinson, Redaktion

MP3-Dateien

Hinweis: Die MP3-Dateien findest du auf der Plattform MyStark. Du kannst sie über den Zugangscode auf der Umschlaginnenseite freischalten.

Listening Tests 1–10 gesprochen von: Eva Adelseck, Daniel Beaver, Esther Gilvray, Daniel Holzberg, Rees Jeannotte, Daria Kozlova, Barbara Krzoska, Jennifer Mikulla, Julian Powell, Rachel Teear, Benjamin Tendler, Roger Voight

Die **Hintergrundgeräusche** in den Tracks (Listening Tests 1–10) stammen von Freesound, Pacdv und Soundsnap.

Vorwort

Liebe Schülerin, lieber Schüler,

dieses Buch hilft dir bei der selbstständigen und langfristigen Vorbereitung auf Klassenarbeiten und die **Abschlussarbeiten am Ende der 10. Klasse an der IGS (E-Kurs und G-Kurs)** im Fach Englisch.

- Die **Übungsaufgaben** widmen sich den Kompetenzbereichen *Listening*, *Reading*, *Mediating*, *Writing* und *Speaking*. In den ersten Abschnitten erfährst du jeweils, welche Anforderungen auf dich zukommen können und wie du dich am besten darauf vorbereitest. Anhand der Übungen kannst du trainieren, wie man mit möglichen Aufgabenstellungen umgeht und sie erfolgreich löst.
- Im Anschluss findest du die **Original-Prüfungsaufgaben** der letzten Jahre. Damit kannst du deine Kenntnisse „unter Prüfungsbedingungen" testen.
- Eine Auswahl **hilfreicher Wendungen**, die dir in den unterschiedlichsten Bereichen nützlich sein werden, erleichtert dir das selbstständige Verfassen von Texten sowie die Vorbereitung auf die mündliche Prüfung. Diese wichtigen Wortschatzelemente kannst du auch digital üben. Die sogenannten „MindCards", interaktive Vokabelkärtchen, sind für die Arbeit am Smartphone oder Tablet bestens geeignet. Du kannst sie über die QR-Codes oder über die beiden Links einfach und schnell abrufen:
  https://www.stark-verlag.de/mindcards/writing-1
  https://www.stark-verlag.de/mindcards/speaking-1

Writing

Speaking

- Über die Plattform **MyStark** kannst du außerdem auf die **digitalen Inhalte** zu deinem Band zugreifen (Zugangscode vgl. Umschlaginnenseite).
  Hier findest du:
  - die **Original-Prüfungsaufgaben 2023** als PDF,
  - **MP3-Dateien** zu den Hörverstehenstexten der Übungsaufgaben und der Original-Prüfungsaufgaben,
  - **interaktive Aufgaben**, mit denen du sprachliche **Grundlagen** in den Bereichen **Grammatik und Wortschatz** wiederholen kannst**,**
  - eine **digitale Kurzgrammatik**, in der du nachschlagen kannst, wenn du in der Grammatik einmal unsicher bist sowie
  - **Lernvideos** zu wichtigen grammatischen Strukturen und zu Strategien, wie du am besten Vokabeln lernst (auch über QR-Code abrufbar).

Lernvideos

Ein separater Band (Best.-Nr. D03950L) enthält zu allen Aufgaben dieses Buches **ausführliche Lösungsvorschläge** mit **hilfreichen Tipps**.

Viel Spaß beim Üben und viel Erfolg in der Prüfung!

Hinweise zur Abschlussprüfung

Schülerinnen und Schüler der 10. Klassen an der Integrierten Gesamtschule nehmen an den zentralen Prüfungen zum Erwerb des **Sekundarabschlusses I** teil. Die Prüfungsaufgaben werden auf der Grundlage der Kerncurricula für die Integrierte Gesamtschule und der Bildungsstandards erstellt.

Bearbeitungsdauer

Die Bearbeitungszeiten für die schriftlichen Prüfungen wurden vom Kultusministerium festgelegt. Im Fach Englisch beträgt die zur Verfügung stehende Zeit 120 Minuten.

Ablauf der schriftlichen Prüfung

- Die schriftliche Prüfung besteht aus einem sogenannten Pflichtteil und einem Wahlteil.
- Der **Pflichtteil** der Prüfungen 2021 bis 2023 umfasst die Bereiche *Listening* und *Reading*. Der Bereich *Mediating* wurde jedoch in den vergangenen Jahren nicht geprüft. **Erkundige dich unbedingt vorab bei deiner Lehrkraft, welche Bereiche Teil der Abschlussprüfung 2024 sein werden.**
- Der **Wahlteil** besteht aus zwei Aufgabensets zum Bereich *Writing*. Zunächst hast du 15 Minuten Zeit, beide Aufgabensets zum Kompetenzbereich *Writing* zu sichten und dich für ein Aufgabenset zu entscheiden. Das nicht gewählte Set wird wieder abgegeben.
- Erst jetzt beginnt der eigentliche **Prüfungszeitraum** von 120 Minuten.
- Für den Prüfungsteil *Listening* stehen dir ca. 30 Minuten zur Verfügung. Die Länge dieses Prüfungsteils hängt von der Spiellänge der verwendeten Audioquelle ab.
- Für die restlichen Prüfungsteile stehen dann insgesamt noch ca. 90 Minuten zur Verfügung.
- Die Abschlussarbeiten sind in Aufgaben für den **E-Kurs** und den **G-Kurs** unterteilt.
- In allen Teilen der Prüfung darf ein zweisprachiges Wörterbuch verwendet werden.

Sollten nach Erscheinen dieses Bandes noch wichtige Änderungen in der Abschlussprüfung vom Kultusministerium bekannt gegeben werden, findest du aktuelle Informationen dazu auf der Plattform MyStark.

Übungsaufgaben zu den Kompetenzbereichen

1 Listening

Hörverstehenstexte und die dazugehörigen Aufgabenstellungen können sehr unterschiedlich sein. Die Texte, die du im Rahmen von Klassenarbeiten und in deiner Abschlussprüfung zu hören bekommst, spiegeln meist **reale Sprechsituationen** wider, d. h., man kann solche oder ähnliche Texte im „wirklichen Leben" hören. Die Inhalte der Texte können von der Begrüßungsansprache im Flugzeug über Lautsprecheransagen an einem Bahnhof bis hin zu Nachrichtenmeldungen, Radiointerviews oder Alltagsgesprächen reichen. Es kann sich auch einfach um kurze Berichte oder Podcasts zu den unterschiedlichsten Themen handeln. Genauso vielfältig wie die verschiedenen Arten von Hörtexten können auch die Aufgabenstellungen ausfallen. In diesem Kapitel werden dir die häufigsten Textarten und Aufgabenstellungen zum Kompetenzbereich „Listening" vorgestellt.

1.1 Strategien zum Bereich „Listening"

Vorgehen beim Üben

Bevor du dich an die Bearbeitung der Original-Abschlussprüfungen wagst, die in diesem Buch enthalten sind, kannst du anhand der Übungsaufgaben schon einmal Schritt für Schritt für die Prüfung trainieren.
Versuche, wie in der echten Prüfung, die Aufgaben nur durch Zuhören zu bearbeiten. Zu Übungszwecken kannst du dir die Hörverstehenstexte aber ruhig so oft anhören, wie es notwendig ist. Erst wenn du überhaupt nicht auf die richtige Lösung kommst, solltest du die Hörverstehenstexte im Anhang (Kapitel 6) lesen. Bei der Bearbeitung der Übungsaufgaben kannst du wie folgt vorgehen:

- **Lies dir** erst einmal **die Aufgaben durch**. Hast du sie verstanden? Frage dich, ob du die Hörsituation schon erkennst – handelt es sich z. B. um ein Interview? **Unterstreiche die Schlüsselwörter** in der Aufgabenstellung, damit du weißt, worauf du beim Zuhören besonders achten musst. Falls nötig, kannst du auch das Wörterbuch zu Hilfe nehmen. In der Prüfung solltest du es jedoch aufgrund des Zeitaufwands nur sparsam einsetzen.
- **Höre dir den Text** nun **einmal an**, sodass du weißt, worum es geht. Achte wiederum auf Schlüsselwörter (z. B. „o'clock" oder „a.m.", wenn nach der Uhrzeit gefragt wird).
- **Höre dir den Text** jetzt **noch einmal an und bearbeite** dabei **die Aufgaben**. Wenn du den Text noch nicht richtig verstanden hast oder du Probleme beim Lösen der Aufgaben hast, kannst du den Text noch ein drittes oder viertes Mal anhören.
- **Überprüfe deine Antworten** anschließend am besten anhand des zugehörigen Lösungsbuchs.

- Während der Überprüfung solltest du dir einige Fragen stellen: Wie könnte ein Fehler zustande gekommen sein? Habe ich den Hörtext nicht richtig verstanden? Habe ich die Aufgaben nicht richtig verstanden?
- Falls du viele Fehler gemacht hast, ist es hilfreich, wenn du dir die Lösungen im Buch durchliest, während du den Hörtext ein weiteres Mal anhörst. In diesem Fall solltest du den Listening Test nach einiger Zeit wiederholen.
- Versuche, mit der Bearbeitung jeder weiteren Höraufgabe in diesem Buch die Zahl der Hördurchgänge zu reduzieren, bis du bei der in der Prüfung üblichen Anzahl angelangt bist. In der Prüfung werden die Texte in der Regel zweimal vorgespielt.

Ablauf des Prüfungsteils „Listening" in der Abschlussprüfung

Es ist wichtig, dass du für den „Ernstfall" trainierst und die Aufgaben einer Original-Abschlussprüfung am Stück bearbeitest, damit du weißt, was in der Prüfung auf dich zukommt.

Der Hörverstehenstest läuft folgendermaßen ab:

- Die Anweisungen und Texte werden euch vorgespielt. Die Texte hört ihr dabei zweimal.
- Dir wird zuerst Zeit gegeben, dich mit den Arbeitsanweisungen und Aufgaben vertraut zu machen.
- Nun geht der Hörverstehenstest los. Wenn ein Hörtext das erste Mal vorgespielt wird, darfst du die Aufgaben bereits bearbeiten.
- Wenn der Hörtext wiederholt wird, kannst du deine Antworten überprüfen oder noch vervollständigen.
- Zum Schluss wird dir noch einmal Zeit gegeben, alles durchzusehen.

Tipp

Vor dem ersten Hören
- Lies dir die Anweisungen genau durch, damit du weißt, wie die Aufgabe zu bearbeiten ist.
- Unterstreiche die Schlüsselwörter in der Aufgabenstellung.

Beim ersten Hören
- Höre genau zu. Worum geht es im Text?
- Achte beim Hören auch auf Schlüsselwörter.
- Versuche, so viele Aufgaben wie möglich zu lösen.

Beim zweiten Hören
- Die Fragen folgen der Reihenfolge im Text. Wenn du eine Frage beim ersten Hören nicht beantworten konntest, dann versuche, beim zweiten Hören die Stelle im Text zu finden.
- Bearbeite möglichst alle Aufgaben. Auch wenn du die richtige Lösung nicht weißt, kreuze z. B. bei Multiple-Choice-Aufgaben eine Antwort an. Vielleicht liegst du ja richtig.
- Überprüfe deine Antworten noch einmal.

1.2 Häufige Aufgabenstellungen zum Bereich „Listening"

Auswahlaufgabe *(multiple choice)* mit Bildern

Bei diesem Aufgabentyp hörst du mehrere kurze Texte. Meist handelt es sich um Gespräche zwischen zwei Personen, es können aber auch Texte mit nur einem Sprecher oder einer Sprecherin vorkommen. Zu jedem dieser kurzen Hörtexte gibt es eine Aufgabe mit drei Bildern, von denen du das zum Hörtext passende Bild auswählen musst.

Beispiel

Tour guide: The tour starts at quarter to nine every Saturday and Sunday morning. The meeting point is in front of the train station.

Task and solution:

The tour starts at …

A ☑

B ☐

C ☐

Auswahlaufgabe *(multiple choice)*

Hier bekommst du Fragen mit verschiedenen Antworten vorgelegt, oder Satzanfänge und mehrere Möglichkeiten, die Sätze zu vervollständigen. Beachte, dass die Formulierung in der Aufgabe oft anders lautet als im Hörtext.

Beispiel

Tim: I'm sorry I'm late. The bus didn't come so I had to walk home and get my bike.

Task and solution:

Tick (✓) the correct answer.

Why was the man late?

- ☐ Because the bus was late and he cycled.
- ☐ Because he walked.
- ☑ Because there was no bus.

Einsetzaufgabe *(Fill in the missing information)*

Hier musst du fehlende Informationen meist in einer **Tabelle** ergänzen. Es ist aber auch möglich, dass du Sätze vervollständigen oder Formulare ausfüllen sollst. Da bei diesem Aufgabentyp detailgenaues Verstehen gefordert ist, ist es besonders wichtig, dass du die Aufgabenstellung bereits vor dem Hören des Textes aufmerksam durchliest, damit du weißt, worauf du beim Hören achten musst. Manchmal musst du nur ein Wort, manchmal mehrere Wörter und manchmal auch Zahlen eintragen. Arbeite ganz konzentriert, damit du die geforderten Informationen beim Hören nicht verpasst.

Wenn du ein Wort nicht sofort verstehst, grüble nicht darüber nach, sondern versuche, die restlichen Lücken auszufüllen. Dieses eine Wort kannst du beim zweiten Hördurchgang nachtragen.

Beispiel

Speaker: The man's smartphone rang in the bus queue. He turned away to talk. When he turned around, the bus had gone without him.

Task and solution:
Fill in the missing information.

1	As he had turned away to speak on the phone, the man	missed the bus .

True or false?

Bei diesem Aufgabentyp sollst du entscheiden, ob eine Aussage richtig *(true)* oder falsch *(false)* ist. Meist weicht dabei die Formulierung der Aussage in der Aufgabenstellung etwas von derjenigen im Text ab.

Beispiel

Pete: It was forty minutes to the bus station.

Task: Decide whether the statement is *true* or *false*.

Solution: It was a long way to the bus station. true ☑ false ☐

Matching

Eine weitere Aufgabenstellung, die häufig in Klassenarbeiten vorkommt, aber auch Teil der Abschlussprüfung sein könnte, ist *matching*. Bei dieser Aufgabenstellung hörst du häufig kurze Äußerungen verschiedener Personen zu einem Thema, denen du dann die entsprechenden Aussagen *(statements)*, die dir schriftlich vorliegen, zuordnen musst.

Beispiel

Amelia: I think I'd like to see a lot more done for the environment. There's a lot of talking, but where's the action? And when something is suggested, like wind-farms, then people start complaining that they spoil the view!

Ethan: If public transport was better, people would use their cars less and that would mean less pollution and cleaner air in our cities. It's the same with cycle tracks. If there were more car-free routes for bikes, more people would cycle.

Task: Write down the correct speaker for each statement.

a) More should be done to reduce traffic in towns.

b) Most people aren't really willing to do something for the environment.

Solution: a) Ethan

b) Amelia

1.3 Übungsaufgaben zum Bereich „Listening“

Listening Test 1: Short conversations

You will hear seven short recordings.
For each question there is a conversation to listen to and three pictures to look at. Tick (✓) the picture which answers the question.
Listen to the conversations twice.

1. Where does Tom want to go on holiday?

A ☐

B ☐

C ☐

2. What does the man need?

A ☐

B ☐

C ☐

3. How many minutes late is the train today?

A ☐

B ☐

C ☐

4. What did the bird take?

A ☐

B ☐

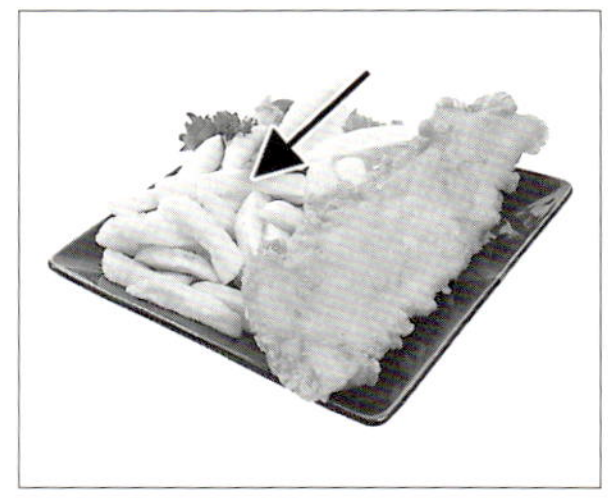

C ☐

5. Which question is difficult?

14

A ☐

15

B ☐

16

C ☐

6. What is Emma going to buy?

A ☐

B ☐

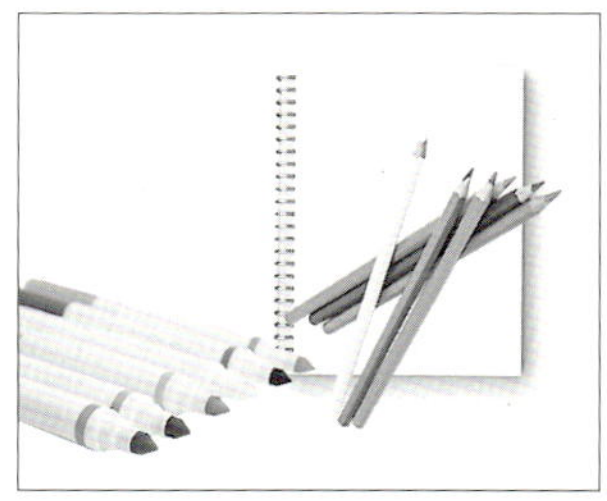

C ☐

7. Which way is lucky?

A ☐

B ☐

C ☐

Listening Test 2: Short texts

You will hear six recordings. There is one question for each recording.
Tick (✓) the correct answer to each question.

1. Which group of people get onto the plane second?

A ☐

B ☐

C ☐

2. How will Daniel get home if his mum can't meet him?

A ☐

B ☐

C ☐

3. Which is the correct way to the hotel?

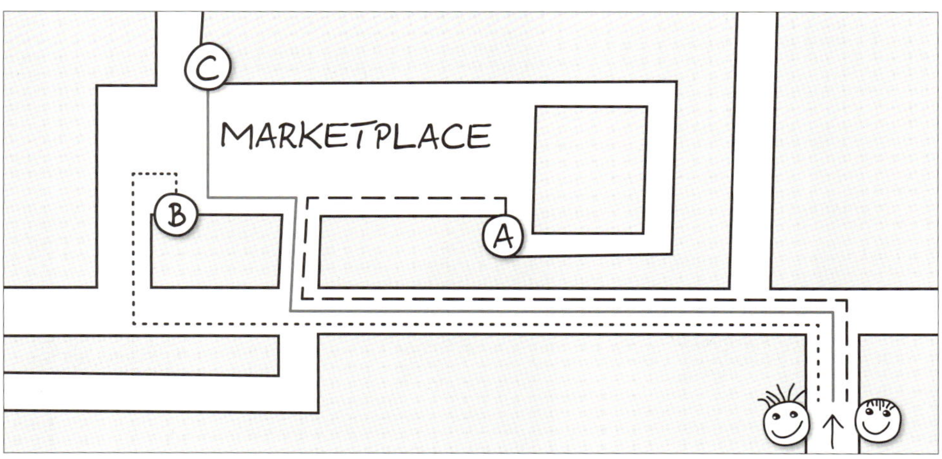

A ☐ B ☐ C ☐

4. What is Tom going to do now on Saturday?

A ☐

B ☐

C ☐

5. Where will each group of friends wait?

A ☐

B ☐

C ☐

6. Where was Lilly when she found out that she'd lost her camera?

A ☐

B ☐

C ☐

Listening Test 3: Sharks

Listen to the conversation between Adam and Nicki about Nicki's experience of sharks. Tick (✓) the correct ending (a, b or c) to each statement (1–7).

1. Nicki's aim after leaving school was to …
   a) enjoy herself. ☐
   b) find a job abroad. ☐
   c) travel the world. ☐

2. Nicki found the shark research …
   a) through a group of people. ☐
   b) by reading about it. ☐
   c) on an advert in school. ☐

3. On her way to Florida, she …
   a) had to help someone. ☐
   b) tried to learn more about sharks. ☐
   c) thought more about her decision. ☐

4. Sharks sometimes attack because …
   a) people and seals often look the same to them. ☐
   b) surfboarders frighten them. ☐
   c) they're hungry and will eat anything. ☐

5. Shark attacks happen but only …
   a) in a few places in the world. ☐
   b) about 18 times every year. ☐
   c) a few people die from them. ☐

6. People are most at risk from …
   a) dogs. ☐
   b) crocodiles. ☐
   c) mosquitoes. ☐

7. The safest time to go into the sea in a shark area is …
   a) after breakfast. ☐
   b) about lunchtime. ☐
   c) after your evening meal. ☐

Listening Test 4: The California Gold Rush

Listen to a television presenter and an expert talking about the California Gold Rush. Tick (✓) the correct ending to each sentence.

a gold nugget

1. The first person to find gold was …
   a) a Native American. ☐
   b) a settler. ☐
   c) an Englishman. ☐

2. The gold nugget was discovered in …
   a) a sawmill. ☐
   b) the hills of California. ☐
   c) a river. ☐

3. On the nugget there are …
   a) teeth marks. ☐
   b) many chips missing. ☐
   c) three tests done. ☐

4. The news about the nugget …
   a) went quickly across America. ☐
   b) was stopped at first by the government. ☐
   c) travelled slowly. ☐

5. People in New York first learnt about gold in California …
   a) through a newspaper article. ☐
   b) from stories about it. ☐
   c) from a member of Congress. ☐

6. People travelling west to seek gold …
   a) usually did not have a family. ☐
   b) often had wrong expectations. ☐
   c) knew they would have to work hard. ☐

7. Van Valen's wife …
   a) moved to California to help her husband. ☐
   b) only earned $ 500 in two years. ☐
   c) had a very difficult life. ☐

8. Most of the gold seekers …
   a) were successful enough to have comfortable lives. ☐
   b) did not make a lot of money. ☐
   c) returned home after a few years. ☐

9. One result of the gold rush was that California …
   a) now appeared on maps. ☐
   b) became very rich. ☐
   c) joined the USA. ☐

Listening Test 5: Route 66

Listen to a report about Route 66 in the USA.
Complete the gaps (1–7) with information from the recording.

The highway is	1. ______________ km long.
The highway wasn't the first, the longest or the	2. ______________.
The dust storms happened during the	3. ______________.
The people who left wanted	4. ______________ life in California.
The 1940s and 50s saw the rise of the	5. ______________ culture.
The new highways were faster and didn't have many	6. ______________.
The places that suffered most were the	7. ______________.

Listening Test 6: Things you didn't know about London

You will hear someone talking about London and some unusual facts about it.
Complete the sentences.

London sees about	1. ______________ visitors a year.
Oslo's present for London is for	2. ______________.
The money from *Peter Pan* goes to a	3. ______________.
The Tube was the world's	4. ______________.
While a station was being made the builders found	5. ______________.
The Shard, a famous building in London, is	6. ______________ high.
Many tall buildings have	7. ______________.

Listening Test 7: Say no to plastic!

Lucy campaigns against plastic waste. Richard Gray from White Rose Radio has invited her into the studio to talk about the issue.
Listen to the interview and decide if each sentence (1–9) is true or false.
Tick (✓) the correct box.

In the radio show it is said that …	true	false
1. … the beach wasn't very clean.	☐	☐
2. … it takes hundreds of years for plastic to decompose *(= sich zersetzen)*.	☐	☐
3. … the materials for the spoon came from China.	☐	☐
4. … the spoon didn't have to travel very far.	☐	☐
5. … in England plastic bags cost 50 pence.	☐	☐
6. … many factories are being built to recycle the cups.	☐	☐
7. … half a million paper cups are thrown away in England every day.	☐	☐
8. … 99 % of paper cups can be recycled.	☐	☐
9. … there are some plans to solve the problem already.	☐	☐

Listening Test 8: Booking a hotel room

1. Listen to two people talking on the phone. Listen to the dialogue twice. Decide whether the following statements are true or false.
Tick (✓) the correct answer.

	true	false
a) The caller wants to book a hotel room near Waverley Station.	☐	☐
b) Her parents know about the trip.	☐	☐
c) Her parents have been married for more than 20 years.	☐	☐
d) The Fringe Festival is in summer.	☐	☐
e) You can see Edinburgh Castle from the hotel room.	☐	☐
f) The room costs £ 165 per person per night.	☐	☐
g) The hotel has usually got special offers in the low season.	☐	☐
h) The hotel only offers breakfast.	☐	☐
i) The hotel sends 12 newsletters a year.	☐	☐

2. Listen to the text one more time and imagine you are the hotel receptionist. While listening to the conversation, take notes.

Old Waverley Hotel, Edinburgh

Receptionist in charge:	a)	Breckenridge
Customer's name:	b)	
Who wants to stay at the hotel?	c)	
Dates:	d)	
Description of the room:	e)	• •
Can I put them on the mailing list?	f)	☐ yes ☐ no
E-mail address:	g)	

Listening Test 9: The Stolen Generations

You will hear a radio interview between the presenter, Greg Masters, and his guest, Jenny Green, talking about Australia's "Stolen Generations".

Decide whether each sentence is true or false. Put a tick (✓) in the correct box.

	true	false
1. The Aboriginal children were taken away from their families up until about 1970.	☐	☐
2. The governments wanted to help Aboriginal people integrate.	☐	☐
3. Most Aboriginal people thought their culture was better than the whites'.	☐	☐
4. Most children were put into homes close to their families.	☐	☐
5. The children had to take new names and speak English.	☐	☐
6. In the homes, Aboriginal children received a good education.	☐	☐
7. The government has never said sorry to the Aboriginal community.	☐	☐
8. The problem has still not been completely solved.	☐	☐

Listening Test 10: Part-time jobs

You will hear a radio show in which three pupils are talking about part-time jobs. Who thinks what? Write the correct name (Lexi, Marc, Leo) next to the statement.
Listen to the interview twice.
Be careful: One statement does not fit. Mark this statement with a cross (✗).

1. ______ — I don't charge too much for my tutorials.

2. ______ — My job is exhausting, but I still like it.

3. ______ — I had to give up my job recently.

4. ______ — I regularly look after three children.

2 Reading

Es gibt viele verschiedene Arten von Texten, wie z. B. Werbetexte, Kochrezepte, Bedienungsanleitungen, Bewerbungsschreiben und Lebensläufe, E-Mails und Briefe, Tagebuch- oder Blogeinträge, Zeitungs- und Zeitschriftenartikel, Interviews, Kritiken und literarische Texte. Ebenso vielfältig wie die Textsorten können auch die Aufgabenstellungen dazu sein. Die Textsorten und Aufgabentypen, die am häufigsten in Klassenarbeiten und in der Abschlussprüfung vorkommen, werden dir hier vorgestellt.

2.1 Strategien zum Bereich „Reading"

Je nachdem, welche Art von Lesetext oder welche Art von Aufgabenstellung du bearbeiten musst, unterscheidet sich die Vorgehensweise. Manchmal musst du die Gesamtaussage des Textes erfassen *(reading for the gist)* und manchmal sollst du Details aus dem Text herausfinden. Du musst dann den Text nach den geforderten Informationen durchforsten (*skimming* oder *scanning*).

Arbeitsschritt 1

Zunächst einmal ist es sinnvoll, den Text an sich ganz genau zu betrachten. Manchmal kannst du bereits am **Layout**, d. h. an der Gestaltung des Textes, erkennen, um welche **Textsorte** es geht. Wenn du weißt, ob der dir vorliegende Text eine Werbeanzeige, ein Zeitungsartikel oder ein Interview ist, dann bist du schon einen Schritt weiter. Da der Bereich „Reading" in der Abschlussprüfung aus mehreren Teilen besteht, kommen darin auch verschiedene Textsorten, wie z. B. Werbeanzeigen und Sachtexte, vor.

Arbeitsschritt 2

Als Nächstes solltest du den **Text** einmal **genau lesen**. Die meisten unbekannten Wörter kannst du ganz leicht aus dem **Sinnzusammenhang erschließen**. Lass dich also nicht aus der Ruhe bringen, wenn dir das eine oder andere Wort unbekannt ist. Schlage nur die Wörter im Wörterbuch nach, die du nicht erschließen kannst, die aber für das Verständnis des Textes wichtig sind. Ganz entscheidend ist, dass du dir bei diesem Arbeitsschritt einen guten **Überblick über den Inhalt** des Textes verschaffst.

Arbeitsschritt 3

Nun solltest du die **Aufgabenstellungen genau lesen**, damit du weißt, unter welchen Aspekten du den Text bearbeiten sollst. Wenn du jetzt den Lesetext im Hinblick auf die jeweiligen Aufgabenstellungen liest, kannst du dabei ganz gezielt wichtige **Schlüsselwörter** bzw. **Textpassagen markieren**, damit du sie bei der Bearbeitung der Aufgaben schnell wiederfindest.

Nun bist du für die Beantwortung der Aufgaben gut gerüstet!

Tipp

- Schaue dir den Lesetext genau an. Kannst du vom Layout auf die Textsorte schließen?
- Lies den Text genau durch und verschaffe dir so einen guten Überblick über den Inhalt.
- Lies die Aufgabenstellungen sorgfältig. Markiere beim nochmaligen Lesen des Textes wichtige Textaussagen im Hinblick auf die Aufgabenstellungen.

2.2 Häufige Aufgabenstellungen zum Bereich „Reading“

True or false

Hier musst du entscheiden, ob **Aussagen** zum Text **richtig** oder **falsch** sind. Es ist wichtig, dass du sowohl den Text als auch die „statements“ genau liest, denn ein einziges Wort kann ausschlaggebend dafür sein, ob ein Satz korrekt ist oder nicht. Manchmal wird darüber hinaus von dir verlangt, dass du deine Entscheidung belegst. Du musst dann in der Regel die betreffenden Zeilen angeben.
Der Aufgabentyp „true or false“ kommt in der Abschlussprüfung oft in Verbindung mit mehreren Werbeanzeigen, aber auch mit Sachtexten vor.

Beispiel

Text: The first U.S. American boot camp for teenagers was created in the 1980s to reduce the number of young criminals.

Task: Decide whether the following statement is true or false.

Statement: Boot camps have existed in the USA for about 15 years. true ☐ false ☑

Matching

Es gibt verschiedene Arten von Zuordnungsaufgaben. Häufig sollst du einzelnen Textabschnitten eine passende Überschrift zuordnen oder umgekehrt: Dir werden Überschriften vorgegeben, zu denen du passende Abschnitte im Text finden musst. Manchmal musst du auch verschiedenen Personen, Ländern, Organisationen etc. Informationen oder Aussagen zuordnen.
In der Abschlussprüfung liegen dir meist einige Personenbeschreibungen vor. Du sollst diesen Personen dann einzelne kurze Texte oder Textabschnitte zuordnen, in denen es z. B. um Hobbys, Nebenjobs oder Reiseziele geht. Fast immer ist es so, dass mehr Auswahlmöglichkeiten als Personen vorgegeben sind – du musst also ganz genau hinsehen und darfst dich nicht in die Irre führen lassen.

Beispiel

Text:
① Harry studies English literature at university. He likes the theatre but he doesn't like musicals or comedy very much. One of his favourite plays is coming to London soon so he and a few friends are going to watch it.
② Sam …
③ Kim …

A Macbeth **B** The Lion King **C** The Phantom of the Opera

Task: Match each person (e. g. ① – ③) to the show they are going to watch (e. g. A – C).

Answer:

Harry	Sam	Kim
A	…	…

Multiple choice

Bei diesem Aufgabentyp werden dir der Anfang eines Satzes und **verschiedene Satzenden** oder Fragen mit mehreren Antwortmöglichkeiten vorgegeben. Aus diesen Möglichkeiten musst du diejenige auswählen, die am besten zum Inhalt des Textes passt, und **das richtige Kästchen abhaken**. Oft wird in der Aufgabe nicht genau dieselbe Formulierung verwendet wie im Text; du musst also nach Schlüsselwörtern mit einer ähnlichen Bedeutung suchen und den Text und die Wahlmöglichkeiten genau vergleichen.

Beispiel

Text: In South Africa, young people born after 1994 – the year when Nelson Mandela was elected the first black president – are often referred to as "born frees". They are the first generation to grow up in a free and democratic society, the first who no longer experienced the system of racial segregation that had characterised South Africa for almost half a century.

Task and answer: Tick (✓) the correct box.
"Born frees" …
☐ are young people who were born in 1993 or earlier.
☐ never knew Nelson Mandela in their lifetime.
☑ were born when racial segregation had already been abolished.

Short answers / Filling in gaps

Manchmal sollst du auch Fragen zum Text beantworten oder Beispiele für bestimmte Sachverhalte aus dem Text heraussuchen. Lies den Text bezüglich der Aufgabenstellung aufmerksam durch und markiere die entsprechenden Textstellen. Meist reicht es, wenn du in Stichpunkten antwortest, gelegentlich musst du aber auch einen ganzen Satz formulieren. Es kann auch vorkommen, dass bereits ein Satz vorgegeben ist und du nur eine Lücke vervollständigen musst. Lies also die Aufgabenstellung ganz genau und halte dich an die Vorgaben.

Beispiel

Text: Many projects for volunteers in Australia focus on the protection of wildlife, such as looking after endangered animals like the tree kangaroo or the southern hairy-nosed wombat. By collecting rubbish or planting trees, volunteers can help to restore the typical living space of these species.

Task and answer: What can volunteers do to protect the living space of endangered species? Give two examples from the text:

- ▶ collect rubbish
- ▶ plant trees

2.3 Übungsaufgaben zum Bereich „Reading"

Reading Test 1: A birthday present

Holly and Luke are looking for a birthday present for their mum, who is adventurous, but not very good at sports. Read the adverts carefully, then decide if each statement is true or false. Tick (✓) the correct box.

1

THE Mountain Bike Experience

Four different levels of tracks to follow:
blue for **beginners** to **black** for **experienced mountain bikers**.

- Bikes can be hired by the hour or by the day.
- We even have a limited number of e-mountain bikes (booking in advance).

To book in advance, send an **e-mail** to: info@forestbikes_centre.uk
Phone: 09765/45670

Price: £ 3.50 (hour) / £ 20 (day)
Open: April 1st until November 15th – 10 a.m. to 6 p.m.

2

Back to the Wild

With our experienced leaders, you'll learn how to camp without a tent and what to cook without going to the supermarket!

Interested? Phone **0379/232323** today for a brochure with all the details, dates and prices, or look on our website: www.bewild_hillside.co.uk

3

Every weekend in July and August
we offer 30-minute

flying experiences

in the afternoons
from 1 p.m. – 6 p.m.

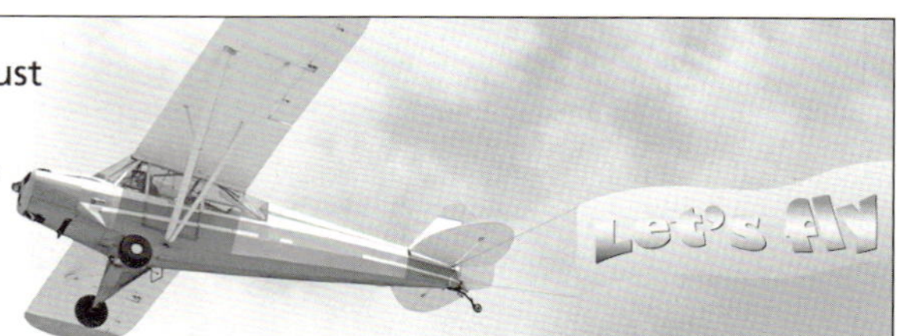

It's a great present for someone – or something just for yourself.
Whatever the reason, book now! It'll be the best 30 minutes of your week!

Each plane can take 1–3 people. Price per take-off: £ 40
Phone the airport and ask for Sabrina.

4

CHOCOLATE DAY

Chocolate is beautiful! Listen to the history of how chocolate came to Britain and watch how we do wonderful things with it. Then try making any chocolate fantasy you have yourself – from a **chocolate handbag** to **chocolate-covered strawberries**!

Phone: Jenny and Jason on 0921/39678 to book a place on the "Chocolate dream course" or fill in the form on our website: **www.chocfan.smallbusiness.com**

	true	false
1. All you need to bring is a tent.	☐	☐
2. It is cheaper if there are three people.	☐	☐
3. E-bikes are available all year.	☐	☐
4. You can only go flying during the week.	☐	☐
5. If you have a dream, you might be able to make it.	☐	☐
6. There is a route for everyone.	☐	☐
7. You will need to bring your own food.	☐	☐
8. You can only phone to book this special present.	☐	☐
9. They show participants what they can do first.	☐	☐
10. Holly and Luke's mum would go on the black track if her birthday present was "The Mountain Bike Experience".	☐	☐

Reading Test 2: What can we do today?

On holiday, the Meyers saw some interesting adverts for different activities and places to visit. Read the adverts on the next page carefully, then decide which of the sentence endings is the correct one for each advert. Put a tick (✓) in the correct box.

1. You can't go sky walking …
   a) if you are over 16 years old. ☐
   b) if it is raining. ☐
   c) if you are 1.90 metres or taller. ☐
2. The Westwood family …
   a) have owned the house for more than 700 years. ☐
   b) know some ghost stories. ☐
   c) offer daily tours of their house. ☐
3. It is possible …
   a) to visit the zoo on a Sunday. ☐
   b) to see polar bears at the zoo. ☐
   c) for children to feed some of the animals. ☐
4. You …
   a) can choose the food for your picnic. ☐
   b) only have to pay £ 150 for a day's driving. ☐
   c) can only rent old cars. ☐

1

Then walk through the treetops! Try our course through the trees at heights of 15 metres above the ground – jump, climb, swing and much more.

Open dry days only:
Daily 9.00 a.m. – 6.00 p.m.
Price: **£ 8.50** – no under 16-year-olds

No booking, just arrive – safety lessons given, and then off you go.

2

Westwood House and Gardens

Lovely 15th-century house with beautiful gardens.

•

Book a visit now and have a tour around the house by the owners, Lord and Lady Westwood.

•

Listen to the stories and see the rooms where people came and made history – ghosts and more.

Open for private tours only. Tel: 0781/5618
Prices: £ 9.45 adults / £ 7.50 children under 16

3

TIGBY ZOO

Enjoy a great day out at Tigby Zoo.

Tigers, lions, bears and lots more – look down on the apes and the monkeys from the treetop walk.
Visit our restaurant; feed the animals in the Children's Corner.

Prices:
£ 12.50 adults
£ 6.50 children under 16

Open: Mon – Sat
9.00 a.m. – 8.00 p.m.

4

Picnic in style

We provide the elegant picnic with homemade food, you choose one of our 20 old cars.

from £ 150 a day (10 hours)

We'll even suggest where to go and what to see.

CARS and more

0716/44552

Reading Test 3: Cities

There are many great cities around the world. Read the information about some of them (A–H). Decide which city each person (1–5) likes. Write the correct letter into the box after each number. You can only use a letter once.

A	**Edinburgh** Take an umbrella! Scotland is often wet, but Edinburgh has lots to offer its visitors. There's a wonderful castle on top of a hill, nice shops, bagpipe players in the streets and much more. One great thing about the city is that the station is in the middle of it. In a few minutes you can be off your train and in the centre of Edinburgh.
B	**San Francisco** San Francisco isn't very hot even in summer but it's a fun city. You can see the Golden Gate Bridge, watch the seals playing in the harbour at Pier 39 or take a tour of the prison island, Alcatraz. But if you drive, take care – there are lots of very steep roads in the city.
C	**Paris** People find Paris romantic. It's got beautiful buildings, wide streets and open spaces. It's an elegant city with lots of museums and famous sights, such as the Eiffel Tower or Notre Dame Cathedral. You can take a boat tour on the River Seine or just sit in a street café and watch people.
D	**London** London is exciting and full of life. Everything you want is there: great theatres and museums, lots of shops and sights to see. It's also full of red double-decker buses and black taxis. Lots of famous people live in London, so maybe you'll see someone you know.
E	**Munich** Munich is a nice city to visit with lots of museums, art galleries, shops, parks and many other things. Of course, it's famous for its 'Oktoberfest' and its Christmas markets – and its football team. But there is one thing every visitor must try in Munich and that's 'Weißwürste'!
F	**New York** New York is famous for its skyscrapers, the Statue of Liberty, yellow taxis and Central Park. But there is much more to see and do in New York, including a Broadway play in the evening. New York's nickname is 'The Big Apple' but no one really knows why it's called that!
G	**Rome** Pizza, pasta and ice cream. Rome has it all and the original versions! Of course, there is more to Rome than food. Around every street corner there is an ancient building. Walk where Julius Caesar walked or visit the Colosseum where huge crowds watched gladiators fight – and if you get tired of all of Rome's history then go shopping!
H	**Barcelona** Barcelona has a great football team! But there is much more to the city than just sport. It's elegant with many beautiful buildings and an amazing cathedral. It's also got beaches and a cool harbour where lots of rich people have their expensive boats. Barcelona is always worth a visit.

1. ☐ 

Lilly: I like history and so I come here a lot. Every time I visit the city, I see something new – I mean old, but new for me. There's another reason I like coming here: the food is great – far better than what I get at home.

2. ☐ 

Kathy: I don't like lots of sun or flying very far, so I often get on a train and go there – and I know I won't need my sun cream or my passport! I enjoy the atmosphere and the sounds of the city. It's a great place to visit for weekends.

3. ☐ 

Simon: I like to go far away from England. When you're young, you should explore the world. What I like about here is not only the famous sights and the high-rise buildings, but that there is always lots to do during the day and in the evening – and everyone speaks English!

4. ☐ 

Gemma: When I go somewhere, I want the city to have lots of different things in it. I don't just want theatres and sights. I love this city because it has everything: I can go sightseeing in the morning, swimming in the sea in the afternoon and maybe even watch a football match in the evening.

5. ☐ 

Charlie: The weather in this city is not always pleasant, but it can be nice and warm there in summer. I like all the attractions the city has and sometimes I visit it in the autumn and winter for the special events – and I can also eat something that I can't eat at home.

Reading Test 4: The mystery of the Mary Celeste

Read the following story. Then match the first parts of the sentences (1–8) with the sentence endings (A–I).

What happened to the ship called the Mary Celeste? People have been trying to answer this question for more than 100 years. The Mary Celeste was a sailing ship. It was carrying 1,701 barrels of industrial alcohol – not the type of alcohol you drink. It was going from New York to Genoa in Italy. There were seven sailors, the captain, his wife and their two-year-old daughter on board. All the men were good sailors and had a lot of experience. They sailed from New York on 7th November, 1872.

On 4th December, between the coast of Portugal and a group of islands in the Atlantic Ocean, another ship saw the Mary Celeste coming towards it in a strange way. The captain sent two of his men to climb onto the Mary Celeste to see what was wrong. They did, but there was no one on it.

There were more surprises, too: the alcohol was still there, there weren't any signs of a fight, there was a lot of food, and the crew's belongings were still there, too – only the lifeboat was missing, and the ship's papers and navigational instruments. The sails were in bad condition, and there was some water inside the ship, but it was not seriously damaged. The ship's diary had been completed every day until 25th November, nine days earlier.

The men who found the ship sailed to Gibraltar in it and left it there. The captain of the Mary Celeste, his family and his men have never been found. What happened to them and why they got off the ship is still a mystery.

		A	in the autumn.
1	No one knows	B	was found by another ship.
2	When the ship left,	C	heavily damaged.
3	All the men on the ship had	D	the true story.
4	The Mary Celeste left America	E	taken their personal things with them.
5	The Mary Celeste	F	was found on 25th November, 1872.
6	There was nobody	G	sailed many times before.
7	No one had	H	on the ship when it was found.
8	The ship was not	I	there were ten people on it.

1	2	3	4	5	6	7	8

Reading Test 5: "We may be 'born free', but …"

Read the article published in a youth magazine and then tick (✓) the correct sentence endings. There is only one correct solution for each statement.

In South Africa, young people born after 1994 – the year when Nelson Rolihlahla Mandela was elected the first black president – are often referred to as "born frees". They are the first generation to grow up in a free and democratic society, the first who no longer experienced the system of racial segregation that had characterised South Africa for almost half a century.

Sign from the apartheid era in South Africa

During the so-called apartheid era, the population was divided into the following four racial groups: White, Bantu (black Africans), Coloured (of mixed ethnic origin) and Asian. While people with British or Dutch roots enjoyed lots of privileges, the non-white groups (especially black people) were systematically oppressed. For example, they were not allowed to vote and were forced to live in particular areas called "homelands". Public facilities were usually segregated into white and non-white zones so that white people didn't have to share the same space with members of the other groups.

For "born frees" like Mbali Legodi, a black young woman from Cape Town, this period seems far away. "Of course, my parents and grandparents have often told me about it, but I can't really imagine what it must have been like. I think for most of our generation it's normal to move around freely or be allowed to vote." Young South Africans nowadays take many of the hard-won privileges for granted, which has led some of the older generation to think of the "born frees" as spoiled or naive. Yet today's youngsters have to cope with problems of their own.

"Many of my friends are unemployed, there simply aren't enough jobs," Mbali says. According to recent statistics, about 60 per cent of South Africans between the ages of 15 and 24 are out of work. Black Africans seem to be particularly at risk of facing long-term joblessness. In addition, those who do find work also earn considerably less than the average white person. "I guess if you look at it from that perspective, not so much has changed. Even years after the end of apartheid, the old inequalities are still in place."

Has she ever considered leaving South Africa and moving to another country? "I knew you would ask that. But no, never. I mean, just look around you: I live in the most beautiful country in the world. There are so many creative people, people who want to change things. We may be 'born free', but there's still a lot for us to do in this society."

1. The term “born frees” refers to …
   a) black people who were released from prison. ☐
   b) the children of President Mandela. ☐
   c) South Africans born after the end of apartheid. ☐

2. Through the apartheid system, non-whites …
   a) lost their political voice. ☐
   b) had to live in rural areas. ☐
   c) oppressed other minority groups. ☐

3. A lot of young South Africans …
   a) have no respect for the older generation. ☐
   b) have never even heard of apartheid. ☐
   c) consider it normal to be living in a democratic society. ☐

4. Over half of young South Africans …
   a) earn average wages today. ☐
   b) now have a positive future. ☐
   c) face difficult employment prospects. ☐

5. Today, the inequalities of apartheid …
   a) have completely disappeared. ☐
   b) can still be felt. ☐
   c) have been made illegal. ☐

6. Mbali Legodi wants to …
   a) stay in her country. ☐
   b) start a new life abroad. ☐
   c) study in Europe. ☐

7. Many born frees want to …
   a) build a new South Africa. ☐
   b) leave their country. ☐
   c) create a new lifestyle. ☐

Reading Test 6: Green roofs benefit people

Decide if each sentence is *true* or *false* and where you find the information in the text. Then tick (✓) the correct box and give the lines where you find the information. Both parts of the answer must be correct.

Water is a necessity of life. Rain, especially, helps plants grow and stay green. But too much rain – especially in cities – can lead to flooding. That can cause waste water systems, like sewers, to overflow and send pollutants into rivers and other waterways. To fight the problem, several cities in the United States are starting programs like rooftop gardens.

A team at the University of the District of Columbia in the nation's capital has created a garden on the top of one school building. The garden holds many kinds of plants to help absorb rainwater … and grow food at the same time. Rainwater is collected in large containers and sent through a system that waters the rooftop garden. The roof is filled with green life that appeals to insects.

A rooftop garden

In cities, "you don't have that many spaces to choose from and so rooftops are just (unused) space," says Caitlin Arlotta. She is a student in the school's Urban Agriculture program.

The project is part of a research program to see which plants do well on rooftops. The researchers are looking at plants including strawberries, tomatoes and sweet potatoes. "We have the same experiment running with tomatoes as we do with strawberries, so we're doing variety trials and we're trying just to see which variety grows the best in a green roof setting."

One goal of the program is food justice; or in Arlotta's words, "bringing fresh food into cities where you wouldn't necessarily have that access." And that includes produce that might be more used by immigrants. "In the U.S., it may not seem very common to use hibiscus leaves and sweet potato leaves as food, but in many places around the world it is."

Sandy Farber Bandier helps run UDC's Master Gardener program. It seeks to improve cities and make them beautiful by training people to become Master Gardeners. She says she's been surprised by the garden's output. "My biggest surprise was that we produced 4,250 pounds of produce the first year and were able to give that to people in need."

She likes being able to show people who live in D.C. and others beyond the nation's capital what – and how – food can be grown on a rooftop. "This is the future for food.

Abridged and adapted from: Julie Taboh, Susan Shand and Caty Weaver: Green roofs benefit people, in: Voice of America Learning English

		true	false	line(s)
1.	In the cities, too little rain can cause problems.	☐	☐	________
2.	The plants in the rooftop garden soak up the rain-water.	☐	☐	________
3.	Rainwater cannot be used to grow food in the garden because it is polluted.	☐	☐	________
4.	Animals are attracted by the plants in the rooftop garden.	☐	☐	________
5.	The researchers try to find out what plants grow best on the rooftop.	☐	☐	________
6.	They only want to grow food that is commonly eaten in the United States.	☐	☐	________
7.	Ms Farber Bandier was happy with the amount of food produced in the garden.	☐	☐	________

Reading Test 7: Volunteering in Australia

Read the text about young people doing voluntary work in Australia. Decide if each statement is *true* or *false*. Tick (✓) the correct box "true" or "false" and give the lines in which you can find the relevant information.

Australia has long been one of the top gap-year destinations for young people from around the globe who have just finished school and want to travel for a year before starting a job or continuing their education. Many of them feel they want to do "something useful" during this time and decide to do voluntary work for a few weeks.

There are all sorts of projects in Australia in need of volunteers who are willing to get their hands dirty for a while. Most of those projects focus on the protection of wildlife, such as looking after endangered animals like the tree kangaroo, the flatback sea turtle or the southern hairy-nosed wombat. By collecting rubbish, planting trees or removing plants that do not naturally belong to the Australian landscapes volunteers can help to restore the typical living space of these species[1]. Constructing and maintaining walking trails or building fences in national parks are also very common activities. Sometimes volunteers also get the chance to assist in research programmes, setting up cameras to monitor endangered species, for example.

Some of these volunteers are international travellers, but Australia is also known as a nation of volunteers with 38 % of women and 34 % of Australian men volunteering regularly. Apart from spending an adventurous time and making new friends, many volunteers also cherish the feeling of learning something about the environment and contributing to its protection. Amber, from Arizona, says, "This program has taught me a great deal about conservation and what it takes to keep parts of a country safe for animals and plants. Life is too precious not to help the world and give something back." It is especially young people who set out on a gap year who feel that volunteering also makes a difference to themselves. "I've grown as a person and conquered so many fears," says Maggie from Canada.

1 species – type of plants or animals

	true	false	line(s)
1. Australia attracts the most people taking gap years in the world.	☐	☐	______
2. Many projects are concerned with nature.	☐	☐	______
3. Some areas need to be made suitable for rare species.	☐	☐	______
4. Volunteers are used to create national parks.	☐	☐	______
5. Volunteers have to take photographs of animals as part of their job.	☐	☐	______
6. Not all volunteers are from abroad.	☐	☐	______
7. Meeting other young people and having fun is an extra benefit of the projects.	☐	☐	______
8. Gaining self-confidence is another result of volunteering during a gap year.	☐	☐	______

3 Mediating

Was versteht man unter „Mediating“? Eine „Mediating“-Aufgabe ist eine Sprachmittlung, d. h., du erhältst einen Text (oder mehrere kurze Texte) auf Englisch oder Deutsch. Deine Aufgabe ist es, den Textinhalt zu verstehen und wichtige Informationen in die jeweils andere Sprache zu übertragen: Du musst also Informationen eines englischen Textes auf Deutsch bzw. bestimmte Details eines deutschen Textes auf Englisch wiedergeben. Häufig sollst du Fragen zu den Texten beantworten oder anderen Personen in einem Gespräch über den Textinhalt berichten. Manchmal musst du auch zwischen zwei Personen, die sich nicht verständigen können, dolmetschen. Aber Achtung: „Mediating“ ist keine wörtliche Übersetzung!

3.1 Strategien zum Bereich „Mediating“

- **Lies die Arbeitsanweisungen und die Texte aufmerksam** durch. Halte dich bei der Bearbeitung der Aufgaben genau an die Vorgaben.
- Denke daran, dass es nicht deine Aufgabe ist, wortwörtlich zu übersetzen! Stattdessen sollst du die relevanten **Informationen sinngemäß** in eine andere Sprache **übertragen**. Gerate deshalb nicht in Panik, wenn du einmal die genaue Bedeutung eines englischen Wortes nicht kennst. Versuche einfach, aus dem Zusammenhang herauszufinden, was gemeint ist.
- Wenn du auf Englisch schreibst, formuliere keine zu komplizierten Sätze; so kannst du unnötige Fehler vermeiden. Denke aber daran, vollständige Sätze zu schreiben, es sei denn, die Arbeitsanweisungen verlangen etwas anderes.
- Liegt dir ein deutscher Text vor, der schwierige Wörter enthält, die du auf Englisch nicht weißt, umschreibe deren Bedeutung oder formuliere deinen Satz so, dass du die unbekannte Vokabel gar nicht brauchst. Lasse jedoch keinesfalls eine Lücke.
- Denke daran, dass die Satzstellung im Englischen von der im Deutschen abweichen kann.
  Die englische Wortstellung in einem Aussagesatz ist *subject – verb – object*.
- Antworten auf Deutsch geben zu müssen klingt leicht, aber viele Schüler und Schülerinnen machen auch im Deutschen Fehler. Beantworte die Fragen in gutem Deutsch und lies anschließend das, was du geschrieben hast, noch einmal aufmerksam durch.
- Dolmetschst du in einem Gespräch, achte auf die richtige Perspektive. Wenn z. B. eine Person von sich selbst spricht, verwendet sie die 1. Person. Wenn du nun einer weiteren Gesprächsteilnehmerin oder einem weiteren Gesprächsteilnehmer über diese Person berichtest, musst du die 3. Person verwenden. Es ändert sich also u. a. das Personalpronomen.

- Achte darauf, dass in einem Gespräch deine Äußerungen zu den vorhergehenden und nachfolgenden Gesprächsbeiträgen passen müssen. Lies also am Ende den gesamten Dialog noch einmal durch und überprüfe, ob deine Lösungen im Zusammenhang einen Sinn ergeben.
- Deine Äußerungen sollen **adressatengerecht** sein – überlege also genau, mit wem du sprichst bzw. für welche Person du einen Text zusammenfasst. Du wirst z. B. deiner kleinen Schwester oder deinem kleinen Bruder Dinge auf andere Art und Weise erklären müssen als beispielsweise deinen Großeltern.
- Wenn dir eine Übung große Schwierigkeiten bereitet, schaue dir im zugehörigen Lösungsbuch die Beispielantworten an. Wiederhole diese Übung dann zu einem späteren Zeitpunkt.

Tipp

- Lies die Arbeitsanweisungen und den Text genau. Markiere ggf. wichtige Textabschnitte in Farbe.
- Beim „Mediating" sollst du nicht wortwörtlich übersetzen, sondern bestimmte Informationen sinngemäß und adressatengerecht in die jeweils andere Sprache übertragen.
- Achte auf einen guten sprachlichen Ausdruck sowie Fehlerfreiheit.
- Lies dir deinen Text oder den vervollständigten Dialog am Ende noch einmal durch und kontrolliere, ob alle gefragten Informationen enthalten sind.

3.2 Häufige Aufgabenstellungen zum Bereich „Mediating"

Die Übungen in diesem Kapitel sollen dir helfen, mit den deutschen und englischen Texten und den jeweiligen Aufgabenformaten umzugehen.
Grundsätzlich unterscheidet man zwischen Sach- und Gebrauchstexten. Im Bereich „Mediating" können dir beide Arten von Texten begegnen. Häufig wirst du dich jedoch mit **Gebrauchstexten**, wie z. B. mit Schildern, Formularen, Werbetexten/Anzeigen, Informationsbroschüren oder Mitteilungen, auseinandersetzen müssen. Auch Alltagsgespräche, Interviews oder Chats sind typische Texte für Sprachmittlungen. Die Arbeitsanweisungen können auf Deutsch oder Englisch formuliert sein.

Im Folgenden stellen wir dir die häufigsten Aufgabenformate vor.

Informationen aus einem Text in einer anderen Sprache zusammenfassen

Deine Aufgabe kann es sein, relevante Informationen aus einem Text in der jeweils anderen Sprache zusammenzufassen. Lies die Aufgabenstellung genau, denn sie kann wichtige Informationen enthalten, für wen du einen Text zusammenfassen musst. Es ist ein Unterschied, ob du einem kleinen Kind oder einem Erwachsenen etwas erklärst.

Beispiel

Text:

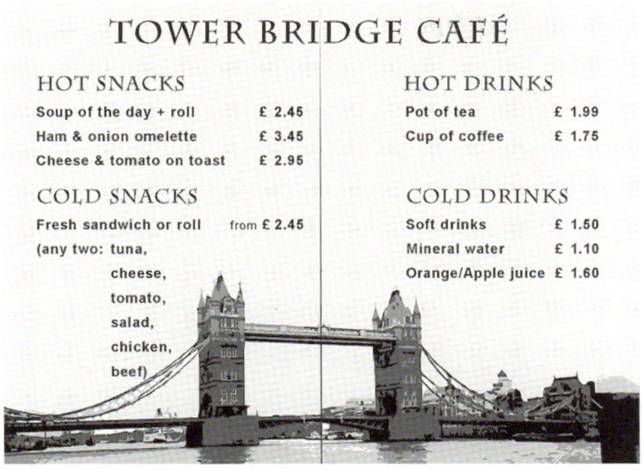

TOWER BRIDGE CAFÉ

HOT SNACKS		HOT DRINKS	
Soup of the day + roll	£ 2.45	Pot of tea	£ 1.99
Ham & onion omelette	£ 3.45	Cup of coffee	£ 1.75
Cheese & tomato on toast	£ 2.95		
COLD SNACKS		**COLD DRINKS**	
Fresh sandwich or roll (any two: tuna, cheese, tomato, salad, chicken, beef)	from £ 2.45	Soft drinks	£ 1.50
		Mineral water	£ 1.10
		Orange/Apple juice	£ 1.60

Task: Du gehst mit deiner kleinen Schwester in ein Café, während deine Eltern noch ein Museum in London besuchen. Erkläre deiner Schwester, was auf der Speisekarte steht, und sage auch, was du gerne essen möchtest.

Answer: Es gibt heiße und kalte Kleinigkeiten, aber keine große Auswahl. Es gibt …

Auf Grundlage eines Textes ein Gespräch vervollständigen

Oftmals sollst du konkrete Fragen zu einem Text beantworten. Achte dabei darauf, dass du auf alle gefragten Aspekte eingehst und dass deine Äußerungen in den Sinnzusammenhang des Gesprächs passen. Meist liegt dir ein deutschsprachiger Text vor, zu dem du ein Gespräch auf Englisch vervollständigen oder Fragen beantworten sollst. Es kommt aber auch vor, dass du zu einem englischen Text einen Dialog auf Deutsch ergänzen oder deutschsprachige Fragen beantworten sollst.

Beispiel

Text:

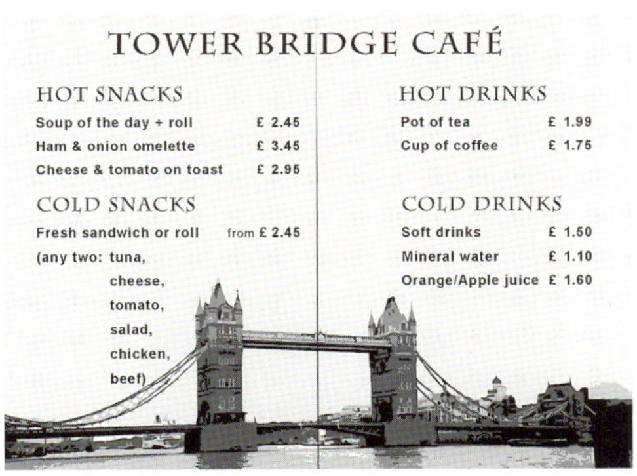

TOWER BRIDGE CAFÉ

HOT SNACKS		HOT DRINKS	
Soup of the day + roll	£ 2.45	Pot of tea	£ 1.99
Ham & onion omelette	£ 3.45	Cup of coffee	£ 1.75
Cheese & tomato on toast	£ 2.95		
COLD SNACKS		**COLD DRINKS**	
Fresh sandwich or roll (any two: tuna, cheese, tomato, salad, chicken, beef)	from £ 2.45	Soft drinks	£ 1.50
		Mineral water	£ 1.10
		Orange/Apple juice	£ 1.60

Task: Du gehst mit deiner kleinen Schwester in ein Café, während deine Eltern noch ein Museum in London besuchen. Beantworte die Fragen deiner Schwester mithilfe der Speisekarte.

Answer:

Schwester: Ich habe großen Hunger. Was gibt es hier denn alles zu essen?

Du: Es gibt nur Kleinigkeiten, aber wir finden bestimmt etwas für dich. Sie haben warme und kalte Gerichte.

Schwester: Mich friert es total. Ich hätte lieber etwas Warmes. Und du weißt ja, dass ich keinen Käse mag.

Du: Es gibt eine Tagessuppe …

In einem Gespräch dolmetschen

Hier wird von dir verlangt, dass du zwischen zwei Personen, die sich nicht miteinander verständigen können, dolmetschst, d. h., du musst Informationen oder Fragen sowohl vom Englischen ins Deutsche als auch vom Deutschen ins Englische übertragen. Denke hier an die richtige Perspektive und passe z. B. die Pronomen an.

Beispiel

Task: Du bist in einem Café in London. Am Nebentisch sitzt ein deutsches Ehepaar, das Schwierigkeiten bei der Bestellung hat. Du bietest deine Hilfe an. Vervollständige das Gespräch.

Answer: **Du:** Entschuldigen Sie, kann ich Ihnen helfen?

Frau: Das ist sehr nett von dir. Ich habe unsere Kellnerin leider nicht verstanden. Könntest du bitte nachfragen, was sie gesagt hat?

Du (zur Kellnerin): *Could you say that again, please?*

Kellnerin: Of course. I just said that today's special is a really delicious pumpkin soup.

Du: *Es gibt heute Kürbissuppe. Die Kellnerin sagt, sie sei sehr lecker …*

3.3 Übungsaufgaben zum Bereich „Mediating"

1. Du machst mit deiner Familie eine Rundreise durch die USA. Dein kleiner Bruder versteht noch kein Englisch, also erklärst du ihm, was auf den Schildern steht.

a)

b)

c)

d)

Keep off the ice! Drowning hazard.
Ice may break.

e)

f)

g)

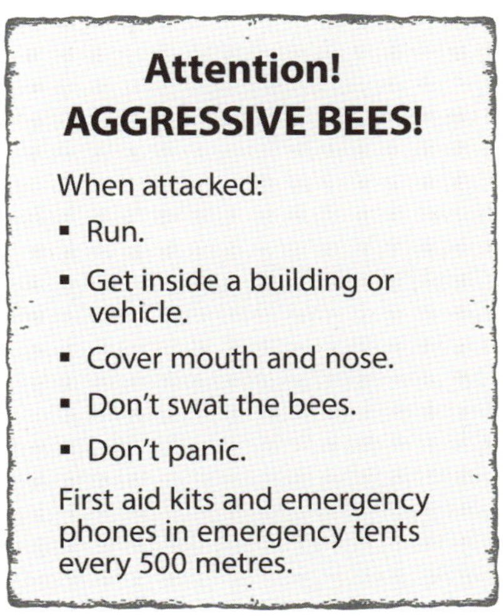

2. During your holiday in England you made a new friend – Julie. A few weeks later, she comes to Germany to visit you. She only speaks English and does not understand the following signs. Explain them to her in English.

a) 

b) 

c) 

d) 

e) 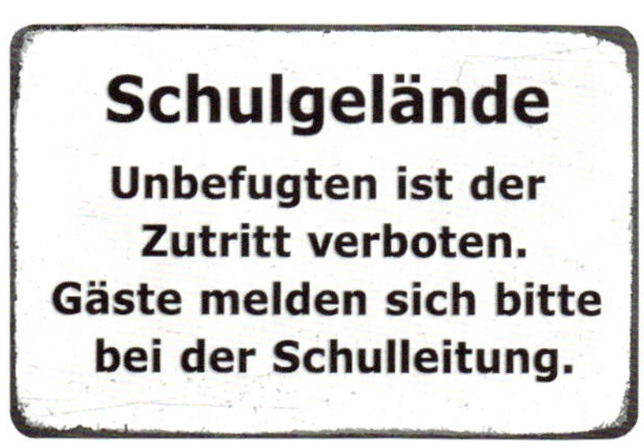

3. Du bist mit deiner Familie gerade in der Nähe von Boston. Dein jüngerer Bruder sieht am 14. Oktober folgendes Plakat und möchte wissen, was darauf steht. Beantworte seine Fragen auf Deutsch.

Bruder: Auf dem Plakat steht etwas von einem Fest, oder? Was ist das für ein Fest?

a) **Du:** ______________________________

____

Bruder: Wann findet es statt? Vielleicht können wir hingehen.

b) **Du:** ______________________________

____

Bruder: Das würde ja klappen. Was gibt es denn auf dem Fest?

c) **Du:** ______________________________

____

____

4. Kim ist Schülerin der River High School. Im Sommer wird sie Besuch von ihrer Freundin Jana aus Deutschland bekommen. Kim möchte in dieser Zeit gerne an einem Wohltätigkeitslauf an ihrer Schule teilnehmen und versucht, Jana dazu zu überreden, auch mitzumachen. Die beiden telefonieren gerade und Kim beantwortet Janas Fragen auf Deutsch.

Running Water

Charity run: 20th August · River High School

We want to raise **$ 10,000** to bring water to the **African village** where our **partner school** is.

Why? Every morning the children have to collect the **day's water** for the family – the well is **5 kms away**. As a result they miss lessons or are very tired at school. If there is water in the village, the children will get a better education because they will have more time to learn.

- **800 m course: people can sponsor each lap up to a maximum of 10 laps**
- **Prize for the most money raised**
- **Food and craft stalls and plenty of extra activities**

If you want to run, please register via email: **runningwater@RHS.org**
For details of how to sponsor someone, visit our website: **www.RHS.org**

Kim: Hi Jana. Ich muss dir etwas erzählen. Ich habe gerade ein Plakat über einen Wohltätigkeitslauf gesehen. Hast du Lust, dass wir beide da mitmachen, wenn du mich besuchst?

Jana: Ein Wohltätigkeitslauf? Das muss ich mir noch überlegen … Wann und wo findet der Lauf denn statt?

a) **Kim:** ______________________________

Jana: OK, an dem Tag wäre ich ja auf jeden Fall schon da. Wofür soll denn Geld gesammelt werden?

b) **Kim:** ______________________________

Jana: Das Dorf hat keine Wasserversorgung? Wo kommt denn das Wasser bisher her?

c) Kim: ______

______

______

Jana: Oje, wenn ich mir vorstelle, ich müsste vor der ersten Stunde so weit gehen … Ich wäre zu nichts zu gebrauchen! Ähm, wie weit müssten wir denn bei dem „Charity Run" laufen?

d) Kim: ______

______

______

Jana: Ein paar Runden würde ich schon schaffen … OK, ich mache auch mit. Muss ich mich irgendwo anmelden?

e) Kim: ______

______

______

5. You see an advert for a great pop festival in your newspaper while your English friend Megan is staying with you. Answer your friend's questions in English.

You: There's a weekend rock festival at Schloss Battenburg. That's near here. Would you like to go?

Megan: That sounds good. Who's playing?

a) **You:** ______________________________

____

Megan: Cool. How much are the tickets?

b) **You:** ______________________________

____

Megan: That's not too bad. If we go for the weekend, where can we stay?

c) **You:** ______________________________

____

Megan: How much is the campsite?

d) **You:** ______________________________

____

Megan: Great. And when does the festival start and finish?

e) **You:** ______________________________

____

Megan: Would we have to take our own food and drink?

f) **You:** ______________________________

____

Megan: Ok, let's go for the weekend!

6. You would like to do a tour of Hamburg harbour with Brandon, and you have found the information on the next page on the internet. Answer Brandon's questions about the tour in English.

   a) A harbor tour sounds great! Where can we get the tickets?

   ____

   ____

   b) Do we have to decide when we want to go?

   ____

   ____

   c) When do the tours take place?

   ____

   ____

   d) I've just turned 16. Do I still get a discount?

   ____

   ____

e) Do they say what we can see on the tour?

Hafenrundfahrt Hamburg

Jetzt buchen – sofort ausdrucken!

Sie erhalten Ihr Ticket für die Hafenrundfahrt mit der Barkasse direkt nach Ihrer Buchung per E-Mail. Drucken Sie das Ticket einfach aus und übergeben es dem Personal am Schiff. Ihr Ticket ist an kein Datum und keine Uhrzeit gebunden. Fahren Sie an Ihrem Wunschtermin!

Tickets für unsere speziellen Touren sind nur online buchbar. Es gibt keine Verkaufsstellen der HTI vor Ort!

Abfahrt täglich: 10:00 – 17:00 UHR – ca. alle 30 Minuten

Preise

Kategorie	Ticketpreis
Erwachsener	18,00 €
Kinder 4 – 14	9,00 €
Kinder 0 – 3	0,00 €

Eigene Darstellung nach https://hamburgtourist.info/hafenrundfahrten/hafenrundfahrt-barkasse-speicherstadt.html; Foto © Can Stock Photo / CarmenSteiner

7. Du nimmst an einem Austauschprogramm teil, bei dem du und dein Partner jeweils drei Monate an der Schule des anderen verbringt. Dein amerikanischer Austauschpartner Sammy hat heute seinen ersten Schultag in Deutschland. Ihr seid im Büro des Schulleiters, der Sammy begrüßen möchte. Da Sammys Deutsch noch nicht so gut ist, dolmetschst du zwischen den beiden.

Schulleiter: *Guten Morgen, ich bin Herr Schwarz, der Schulleiter. Hattest du einen guten Flug?*

a) **You:**

Sammy: Yes, I did, thanks, but it was very long and I'm still a bit tired.

b) **You:**

Schulleiter: Bitte sag ihm, dass ich ihn herzlich an unserer Schule begrüßen möchte und dass ich ihm drei unvergessliche Monate bei uns wünsche. Falls es Probleme geben sollte, kann er sich jederzeit an mich wenden – am besten mit dir als Dolmetscher*in!

c) **You:** ______________________________

____

____

____

Sammy: Oh, that's nice! I hope my German will get better so that I can talk to him without you soon.

d) **You:** ______________________________

____

Nach dem Treffen mit dem Schulleiter gehst du mit Sammy zum Unterricht. Dein Klassenlehrer gibt euch ein Infoblatt zu den Hitzefrei-Regelungen für diese Woche. Lies den Flyer durch und teile Sammy mit, welche Voraussetzung erfüllt sein muss, damit es Hitzefrei gibt und wann die Unterrichtsstunden verkürzt werden.

Liebe Schülerinnen und Schüler,

die erste Hitzewelle des Jahres steht an, daher hier zur Erinnerung die Hitzefrei-Regelungen an unserer Schule:

- Nur wenn die Temperaturen in den Klassenräumen bereits um 10 Uhr morgens die 25 °C-Marke überschreiten, können Unterrichtsstunden ausfallen. Die Temperaturmessung erfolgt an verschiedenen Standorten im Schulgebäude durch den Hausmeister.
- Über den Ausfall von Stunden bestimmen die Schulleiter*innen aller Schulen der Region gemeinsam. Die Abfahrtszeiten der Schulbusse werden koordiniert und entsprechend vorverlegt.
- Liegen die Temperaturen mehrere Tage lang bereits am Vormittag über 25 °C, so werden alle Stunden des Schultages auf 35 Minuten verkürzt. Eine solche Regelung wird ggf. bis spätestens 12 Uhr des Vortages bekannt gegeben.
- Bei extremen Temperaturen und erhöhten Ozonwerten findet kein Sportunterricht im Freien statt. Die Neigungsgruppen Fußball und Leichtathletik müssen dann entfallen, der reguläre Sportunterricht wird in die Sporthalle verlegt.
- Während der Hitzewelle ist das Trinken von Wasser im Unterricht selbstverständlich erlaubt.

gez. Die Schulleitung

e) **You:**

- ______________________________

  ____
- ______________________________

  ____

Sammy: That's cool. At home we have to work in the heat! What about sport?

f) **You:** ______________________________

____

Sammy: Are we allowed to drink in lessons when it is so hot? And how do we get back to your house when the school closes early?

g) **You:**
- ______________________________

  ____
- ______________________________

  ____

8. You and your family are behind an English-speaking tourist at an information desk at Munich airport. The American woman is having language problems since the employee's English is very poor. You decide to help.

You: Can I help? I can speak English and German.

Tourist: Thank you. I'm looking for a typical Bavarian hotel but not in the city.

a) **You:** I'll ask. ______________________________

____

Employee: Das „Hotel Bavaria München" ist sehr gut. Es ist ein wunderschönes Landhotel in der Nähe von München. Hier ist ein Hotelprospekt.
(Der Angestellte gibt dir den Prospekt auf der nächsten Seite).

b) **You:** ______________________________

____

Tourist: That sounds great – and the photos look good, too. Can you ask him if he has the brochure for me in English?

c) **You:** ______________________________

____

Employee: Nein, leider nicht. Die englischsprachigen Prospekte sind aus.

d) The American explains that she's got a rental car but doesn't want to drive into Munich and asks whether it is possible to visit the city using public transport. She'd also like to try some local food but her husband doesn't and they don't want a noisy hotel. Give her the information about these three points from the brochure.

- ______________________________

  ____
- ______________________________

  ____
- ______________________________

  ____

e) Add two more pieces of information which you think are relevant.

- ______________________________
  ____
- ______________________________
  ____

Hotel Bavaria München ☆☆☆

Ankommen und rundum wohlfühlen

Verbringen Sie entspannte Urlaubstage in unserem idyllischen Landhotel, welches dank seiner naturnahen Lage am Stadtrand Münchens viel Ruhe und Erholung bietet.

Dennoch können Sie aufgrund der ausgezeichneten Verkehrsanbindung alle Sehenswürdigkeiten Münchens mit dem Bus oder der S-Bahn bequem und schnell erreichen. Ihr Auto können Sie währenddessen sicher in unserer hoteleigenen Garage lassen.

Kinder dürfen sich auf dem neu errichteten Spielplatz an der frischen Luft austoben und der bestens ausgestattete Fitnessraum kann von unseren erwachsenen Gästen rund um die Uhr genutzt werden.

Unser hauseigenes Restaurant serviert neben internationaler und bayerischer Küche auch vegetarische Gerichte sowie Diätkost. Teilen Sie uns am besten vorab telefonisch Ihre Wünsche mit.

Weitere Informationen und Buchung:

www.hotel-bavaria-munich.de

Tel.: 089/723489

Bezahlen können Sie selbstverständlich bar oder mit Kreditkarte.

9. Your older cousin from Australia, who loves excitement, is visiting you. She was looking at a holiday brochure for things to do near the Baltic coast, because you are going there together for a week. Some photographs of people on quad bikes caught her eye. She wants you to help her understand the German.

Liebst du **DIE GESCHWINDIGKEIT** und das **ABENTEUER** ...

... und möchtest unsere **OSTSEE-INSEL RÜGEN** auf unkonventionelle Art und Weise kennenlernen? Dann bist du bei uns genau richtig!

Komm zu **QUADABENTEUER** und entdecke auf unserer spannenden Offroad-Tour viele wunderschöne und unberührte Orte der größten deutschen Insel – abseits vom Trubel. Mit unseren erfahrenen Guides befährst du eine abwechslungsreiche Strecke, die über Felder, entlang eines Flussbetts, durch Wasser und Schlamm, über steiniges Terrain und Sandstrände führt.

Wenn du Lust hast, dir den Fahrtwind um die Nase wehen zu lassen und Rügen mit dem Quad zu erkunden, schreibe einfach eine kurze E-Mail an:

info@QuadAbenteuer.com

Unsere Mitarbeiterin Marie beantwortet alle deine persönlichen Fragen, z. B. was die Sicherheit, Einweisung, passende Kleidung und Kosten betrifft, zeitnah.

Wir bieten rund ums Jahr Touren für 2 bis 10 Personen an – schlechtes Wetter und Schnee sind kein Hindernis!

Ava: I found some photos of quad biking with something in German about it. It looks great fun. Where do they do this?

a) You: ____________________

Ava: It looks like they go off-road. Can you tell me more?

b) You: ____________________

Ava: That sounds exciting, doesn't it? What happens if it rains?

c) **You:** ______________________________

____

Ava: I wouldn't want to go when it's snowing, but we shouldn't have that problem in August! Is Rügen far away from where we're staying at the Baltic Sea? I'd really love to go quad biking.

You: No, it isn't. Actually, it's only about an hour's drive away, so we can definitely take you there.

Ava: Great! I still have some questions, though. How can I find out more about the quad bike tour?

d) **You:** ______________________________

But would you like me to write the email for you? It's got to be in German, of course.

Ava: Thanks, that'd be great. I'd like to know if they provide everything – clothes and a helmet – or do I need to bring them or anything else? Could you please also ask what time the trips take place and if they take place every day? Oh, I nearly forgot – how much does everything cost and would it be a problem that I don't speak German?

You: No problem – I'll do it now.

e) Du schreibst für Ava eine E-Mail an Marie. Achte darauf, dass du auf alle Fragen von Ava eingehst.

TO: Info@QuadAbenteuer.com

SUBJECT: Fragen zur Quad-Tour

Hallo Marie,

meine Cousine Ava würde gerne im August eine Tour bei *QuadAbenteuer* buchen, aber sie hat vorab noch ein paar Fragen. Es wäre super, wenn Sie die folgenden Fragen beantworten könnten.

____

____

____

____

____

____

____

Herzlichen Dank für die Beantwortung der Fragen.
Viele Grüße und bis bald,
(dein Name)

4 Writing

Viele Schülerinnen und Schüler sind der Meinung, dass sie sich auf den Bereich „Schreiben“ nicht vorbereiten können, da die Aufgabenformen sehr stark variieren und die Note ohnehin stark von der individuellen Einschätzung der Lehrkräfte abhänge. Erschwerend kommt im Fach Englisch noch die Fremdsprache und die damit verbundene Fehleranfälligkeit hinzu. Aus diesen Gründen beschäftigen sich manche Schüler*innen erst gar nicht mit dem Kompetenzbereich „Writing“, was umso schlimmer ist, wenn man bedenkt, dass dieser Bereich rund ein Drittel bis ein Viertel der Note in den meisten Klassenarbeiten und in deiner Abschlussprüfung ausmachen kann.
Mache nicht den gleichen Fehler! Lies die folgenden Seiten gut durch. Du wirst sehen: Eine sinnvolle und erfolgreiche Vorbereitung auf das Schreiben englischer Texte ist möglich. Aus diesem Grund enthält dieser Übungsteil auch vorbereitende Aufgaben, die dir helfen, Texte abwechslungsreicher zu formulieren und beim Schreiben zusammenhängender Texte sicherer zu werden.

4.1 Strategien zum Bereich „Writing“

Langfristige Vorbereitung

Auf das Schreiben von Texten in Klassenarbeiten und in der Abschlussprüfung kannst du dich nur langfristig gut vorbereiten. Wenn du dir erst zwei Tage vor der Prüfung überlegst, dass du in diesem Bereich noch Schwächen hast, dann ist es für eine sinnvolle Beschäftigung mit diesem Thema definitiv zu spät.

Methode 1

Schaue bzw. höre dir englischsprachige Interviews mit deinen Lieblingsstars im Internet (z. B. bei YouTube) oder im Fernsehen an. Sieh dir Filme im Original an, entweder im Kino – falls sie in deiner Stadt im Original vorgeführt werden – oder auf DVD bzw. über einen Streaming-Dienst im Internet (z. B. Netflix). Als Hilfe kannst du dir – falls möglich – auch die englischen Untertitel einblenden lassen und die Dialoge mitlesen.

Methode 2

Versuche, möglichst viel in englischer Sprache zu lesen; auch hier wirst du im Internet fündig. Du kannst dich z. B. über Themen, die dich interessieren, im Online-Lexikon Wikipedia informieren. Hier gibt es übrigens auch den Bereich „Simple English“, falls dir die Texte zu schwierig sind. Oder probiere, Romane und Geschichten auf Englisch zu lesen. Deine Englisch-Lehrkraft kann dir sicher Tipps für geeignete Bücher geben. Du wirst sehen: Mit der Zeit verstehst du mehr und mehr, und viele Ausdrücke und Redewendungen kommen dir immer vertrauter vor, sodass du sie für deine eigenen Texte verwenden kannst.

Methode 3

Eine gute Übung ist es auch, sich viel in der Fremdsprache zu unterhalten. Sprich doch hin und wieder mit deinen Freundinnen oder Freunden bzw. deinen Geschwistern englisch. So wird dir das eigenständige Formulieren von Mal zu Mal leichter fallen.

Wichtig ist also, dass du dich mit der englischen Sprache auch in deiner Freizeit beschäftigst. Dabei geht es nicht nur darum, das Schreiben englischer Texte zu üben, sondern ganz generell sollst du möglichst viel mit dem Englischen in Kontakt kommen. So kannst du deinen Wortschatz erweitern und Sicherheit im Gebrauch der Fremdsprache erwerben, die du zum Verfassen eigener Texte brauchst.

Das Schreiben eines Textes

Es gibt viele verschiedene Arten von Texten, wie z. B. Briefe oder E-Mails, Artikel und Blogs. Ganz gleich, welche Art von Texten du schreiben musst, die Vorgehensweise ist dabei immer ähnlich.

Arbeitsschritt 1 – Aufgabe(n) lesen

Lies die Aufgabenstellung(en) gut durch und überlege genau, was darin von dir verlangt wird. In der Abschlussprüfung sind oft bestimmte Aspekte vorgegeben, die unbedingt in deinen Texten vorkommen müssen. In Klassenarbeiten können die Themen aber auch freier formuliert sein.

Arbeitsschritt 2 – Aufgaben(set) auswählen

Manchmal kannst du in Klassenarbeiten zwischen mehreren Aufgabenstellungen wählen. In deiner Abschlussprüfung musst du mehrere Schreibaufgaben unterschiedlicher Länge verfassen. Du kannst zwischen zwei Aufgabensets, die meist aus jeweils zwei oder drei Aufgaben bestehen, auswählen. **Suche dir die Aufgaben aus, mit denen du dich am besten auskennst.** Vermeide nach Möglichkeit Themen, zu denen du nichts zu sagen hast. Es macht keinen Sinn, einen Brief über deine Abenteuer beim Skifahren zu schreiben, wenn du noch nie etwas mit Wintersport zu tun hattest.
Hast du dich für ein Set entschieden, beginne mit der Aufgabe, bei der du dich am sichersten fühlst. Die Aufgaben steigen im Schwierigkeitsgrad und in der Textlänge bzw. bauen sogar manchmal aufeinander auf, sodass es in der Regel sinnvoll ist, mit der ersten Aufgabe anzufangen.

Arbeitsschritt 3 – Notizen machen

Lies dir die (erste) Aufgabenstellung aufmerksam durch und überlege, was du dazu schreiben könntest. Beachte dabei genau die Vorgaben aus der Aufgabenstellung – die darin genannten Aspekte kannst du meist schon als grobe Gliederung für deinen Text verwenden. Überlege als Nächstes, was du noch hinzufügen musst – fallen dir z. B. schon Beispiele zu den einzelnen Aspekten oder nützliche Formulierungen ein? Dann solltest du sie gleich **auf einem Blatt notieren**. Gleiche deine Notizen anschließend noch einmal mit der Aufgabenstellung ab, um sicherzugehen, dass du wirklich alle geforderten Aspekte berücksichtigt hast.

Arbeitsschritt 4 – Text schreiben

Nun musst du den **Text formulieren**. Gehe dabei Schritt für Schritt die Aufgabenstellung durch und formuliere die einzelnen Sätze aus. Gute inhaltliche Ideen sind dabei genauso wichtig wie ein **klarer Aufbau** deines Textes. Versuche, Abhängigkeiten, Folgen etc. durch entsprechende Konjunktionen, also durch Bindewörter, wie z. B. „because“ oder „although“, deutlich zu machen. Schreibe kurze, überschaubare Sätze; so kannst du Grammatikfehler leichter vermeiden. Achte dennoch darauf, dass du nicht jeden Satz gleich aufbaust, sondern unterschiedliche Strukturen verwendest. Auch beim Wortschatz solltest du abwechseln, d. h. nicht immer die gleichen Wörter wiederholen. Greife auf Redewendungen zurück, die du gelernt hast. Wenn du etwas nicht ausdrücken kannst oder dir der Wortschatz fehlt, dann versuche, die Begriffe zu umschreiben oder notfalls einen anderen Aspekt zu finden, zu dem dir die Vokabeln leichter einfallen. In Kapitel 4.2 findest du eine Zusammenstellung vieler nützlicher Formulierungen, die dir beim Aufsatzschreiben helfen werden. Lerne sie auswendig. Du wirst sie immer wieder einsetzen können.
Achte auch darauf, in etwa die geforderte **Wortzahl** einzuhalten, da dir ansonsten Punkte abgezogen werden können.

Arbeitsschritt 5 – Text korrigieren

Nimm dir auf jeden Fall die Zeit, **deinen Text** abschließend noch einmal in Ruhe **durchzulesen**. Ist alles logisch aufgebaut? Sind die einzelnen Sätze sinnvoll miteinander verknüpft oder gibt es irgendwo Gedankensprünge? Bist du auf alle in der Aufgabenstellung genannten Aspekte *(prompts)* eingegangen? Wichtig ist auch, dass du noch einmal gezielt nach Rechtschreib- und Grammatikfehlern suchst und diese entsprechend verbesserst.

Vielleicht kommen dir die beschriebenen Arbeitsschritte recht zeitaufwendig und umständlich vor. Versuche aber dennoch, nach diesem Schema vorzugehen: Du wirst merken, dass dir das bei den Hausaufgaben, in Klassenarbeiten und natürlich erst recht in der Prüfung wertvolle Zeit spart. So wird es kaum passieren, dass du eine falsche Aufgabe oder ein Aufgabenset auswählst, das dir nicht liegt, und das erst merkst, wenn du schon mitten im Schreiben bist. Klar sollte dir allerdings auch sein, dass du dieses Verfahren üben musst.

Tipp

- Lies die Aufgabenstellung(en) genau und analysiere sie.
- Wähle die für dich geeignete(n) Aufgabe(n) aus.
- Notiere dir zu der Aufgabe, die du zuerst bearbeiten möchtest, einige Stichpunkte.
- Überprüfe, ob du alle Aspekte der Aufgabenstellung berücksichtigt hast.
- Formuliere den Text anhand der Aufgabenstellung und der vorgegebenen *prompts* Schritt für Schritt aus.
- Lies deinen Text abschließend noch einmal genau durch und überprüfe dabei, ob alles logisch aufgebaut und verständlich geschrieben ist. Verbessere Rechtschreib- und Grammatikfehler.
- Gehe bei allen weiteren Schreibaufgaben genauso vor.

Writing

4.2 Hilfreiche Wendungen

Die folgenden Wörter und Ausdrücke helfen dir beim Schreiben von Texten. Du solltest sie auswendig lernen. Die Wendungen sind übrigens auch als digitale „MindCards“ verfügbar, mit denen du am Smartphone oder Tablet üben kannst.

Formulierungshilfen für E-Mails und Briefe

Anrede und Schlussformeln in formellen E-Mails und Briefen (z. B. Geschäftsbrief / Anfrage)

wenn du den Namen der Ansprechperson nicht kennst:

Sehr geehrte Damen und Herren,	*Dear Sir / Madam,* *Dear Sir or Madam,* *To whom it may concern:*
Mit freundlichen Grüßen	*Yours faithfully,*

wenn du den Namen der Ansprechperson kennst:

Sehr geehrte Frau Roberts,	*Dear Mrs Roberts,*
Sehr geehrter Herr James,	*Dear Mr James,*
wenn du nicht weißt, ob die Frau verheiratet ist oder nicht	*Dear Ms Bell,*
Mit freundlichen Grüßen	*Yours sincerely,*

Layout eines Geschäftsbriefes

24 Castle Street Blackburn Lancashire LK6 5TQ	Absender (ohne Namen)[1]
6th March 20…	Datum[2]
Mrs J. Fox Dane Cleaners 3 Arthur Road Doddington NE3 6LD	Name + Adresse des Empfängers (bei Geschäfts-briefen)
Dear Mrs Fox,	Anrede
Thank you for your letter …	
Yours sincerely,	Schlussformel
Adam Smith	Unterschrift
Adam Smith	Name

1 Die Adresse des Absenders kann auch auf der linken Seite stehen.

2 Das Datum kann auch links stehen. Die Schreibweisen 6 March 20… / March 6, 20… / March 6th, 20… sind alternativ möglich.

Tipp

In formellen E-Mails und Briefen musst du die Langformen der Verben verwenden (z. B. „I am“ anstelle von „I'm“).

Anrede und Schlussformeln in persönlichen E-Mails und Briefen

Liebe Jane,	Dear Jane,
Viele Grüße/Liebe Grüße	Best wishes, Love, *(nur bei sehr guten Freunden; von Frauen viel häufiger verwendet als von Männern)*

Mögliche Einleitungs- und Schlusssätze

Danke für ...	Thank you for ...
Ich habe ... erhalten.	I received ...
Ich hoffe, dass ...	I hope (that) ...
Wie geht es dir?	How are you?
Im letzten Brief hast du mir von ... erzählt.	In your last letter you told me about ...
Im letzten Brief hast du mir erzählt, dass ...	In your last letter you told me (that) ...
Entschuldige, dass ich ... vergessen habe, aber ...	Sorry that I forgot to ..., but ...
Sage bitte .../Richte ... bitte aus ...	Please tell ...
Es wäre schön, wenn wir uns treffen könnten.	It would be nice if we could meet.
Bitte richte ... (schöne) Grüße aus.	Best wishes to .../ Please give my (best) regards to .../ Please say hi/hello to ... from me.
Bitte schreibe mir bald zurück.	Please write soon.
Ich freue mich darauf, bald von dir zu hören.	I'm looking forward to hearing from you soon./I hope to hear from you soon.
Ich freue mich auf deinen Brief.	I'm looking forward to your letter.
Ich werde dich anrufen.	I'll call/ring you.

Weitere häufig vorkommende Redewendungen/Ausdrücke

sich entschuldigen	I'm sorry ...
etwas bedauern/Enttäuschung ausdrücken	It's a pity that .../ I'm disappointed that .../ I was deeply disappointed by ...
an etwas erinnern	Please remember to ...
Überraschung äußern	I was surprised that ...
eine Bitte äußern	Could/Would you ..., please?

einen Wunsch äußern	I'd like to … / I'd love to …
einen Entschluss mitteilen	I've decided to … / I'm going to … / I've made up my mind to …
eine Absicht mitteilen	I intend to … / I will … / I want to … / I'm planning to …
Interesse ausdrücken	I'm interested in …
Freude ausdrücken	I'm happy / glad about …
Überzeugung ausdrücken	I'm convinced that … / I'm sure that …
nach dem Preis fragen	How much is it? / … does it cost?
Ich hoffe, dir hat … gefallen.	I hope you liked / enjoyed …
Ich muss jetzt …	I have to … now.
Ich denke, es ist besser …	I think it's better to …

Auskunft geben über sich selbst

Ich wohne in …	I live in …
Ich wurde am … in … geboren.	I was born in … on (17th June 2004).
Ich interessiere mich für …	I'm interested in …
Ich war schon in …	I've (already) been in … / to …
Ich möchte gerne … werden.	I'd like to be a / an …
Mir geht es gut.	I'm fine.
Mir geht es nicht gut.	I'm not well. / I don't feel well.
Ich mag …	I like … / I enjoy …
Ich mag … lieber (als …)	I prefer … to … / I like … better (than …)
Ich weiß … noch nicht genau.	I still don't know exactly …
Ich plane, … zu tun.	I plan to …
Ich freue mich (sehr) auf …	I'm (very much) looking forward to … I'm (very) excited about …
Ich konnte nicht …	I wasn't able to … / I couldn't …
In meiner Freizeit …	In my free time / spare time …
Ich nehme regelmäßig an … teil.	I take part in … regularly.

Formulierungshilfen zur Strukturierung von Texten (z. B. für eine persönliche Stellungnahme oder einen Artikel)

einen Text einleiten	To begin with, … First of all, …
einen Text abschließen	To sum up, … / In summary, … / All in all, … To conclude, … / In conclusion, …

Argumente aufzählen	Firstly, … Secondly, … Thirdly, … Finally, …
Argumente gegeneinander abwägen	On the one hand … On the other hand …
auf Widersprüche hinweisen/ etwas einräumen	but however yet although despite / in spite of in contrast to otherwise nevertheless
zusätzliche Aspekte anführen	In addition, … Moreover, … Furthermore, … Not only that, but … Another important point / aspect (to mention) is …
Beispiele geben	for example / e. g. for instance like such as
Gründe anführen	Due to … Thanks to … The reason for this is that … because (of) as since therefore
auf die Folgen von etwas hinweisen	As a result, … Consequently, …
die eigene Meinung ausdrücken	In my opinion / view, … Personally, I think / believe that … To my mind, … As far as I am concerned, … As for me, …
Zweifel/Sorge ausdrücken	I am not quite sure whether … I doubt that … I am concerned / worried that …
Zustimmung ausdrücken	I think so too. I agree with this statement. That is right / correct. I am of the same opinion.

Ablehnung ausdrücken	I do not think so. I do not agree. / I disagree. That is wrong / not correct. I am not of the same opinion.

Verben des Sagens (z. B. für Fantasiegeschichten)

sagen	to say sth / to tell sb sth
fragen	to ask
sich fragen	to ask oneself / to wonder
antworten / erwidern	to answer / to reply / to respond
flüstern	to whisper
murmeln	to murmur / to mutter / to mumble
schreien	to call (out) / to yell / to scream / to shout
erwähnen	to mention

4.3 Häufige Aufgabenstellungen zum Bereich „Writing"

Die Texte, die du in deiner Abschlussprüfung schreiben sollst, sind unterschiedlich lang. In der Regel wird in der Aufgabenstellung eine ganz bestimmte Art von Text von dir verlangt. Die **Textsorten**, die in der Abschlussprüfung vorkommen können, sind **vielfältig:** Du musst z. B. in der Lage sein, kurze Nachrichten, Notizen, Einladungen, Briefe oder E-Mails, Artikel, Einträge in sozialen Netzwerken oder Geschichten zu verfassen, Reviews oder Inserate zu formulieren, Fragen zu stellen, Empfehlungen auszusprechen oder Vergleiche anzustellen. Wichtig ist, dass du deine **Meinung ausdrücken** und zu einem Thema **Stellung nehmen** kannst. Außerdem wird von dir verlangt, **unterschiedliche Perspektiven einzunehmen**. Das bedeutet, dass du immer überlegen musst, in welche Rolle du jeweils schlüpfen sollst, wenn du einen Text schreibst.

Auch die **Themenbereiche sind vielfältig**. Häufig geht es in den Texten um „Urlaub" oder weitläufig um „Schule", aber auch kreative Schreibaufgaben, bei denen du deiner Fantasie freien Lauf lassen kannst, kommen immer wieder vor. In der Regel sind **mehrere Aspekte vorgegeben**, die unbedingt in deiner Lösung enthalten sein müssen. Oftmals erhältst du zusätzliche Informationen, die du in deinen Text einbeziehen musst. Diese Informationen können dir in Form einer Grafik, eines Bildes oder auch eines Textes (z. B. eine E-Mail, eine Nachricht oder ein Zeitungsartikel) vorliegen. Gelegentlich wird dir auch der Anfang des Textes vorgegeben, den du fortsetzen sollst.

Im Folgenden werden die Textsorten, die am häufigsten in der Prüfung vorkommen, näher vorgestellt.

Formulare

Manchmal erhältst du ein Formular, das du ausfüllen musst. Es kann sich z. B. um eine Buchungsanfrage, ein Bewerbungsformular oder eine Registrierung für einen Onlineshop handeln. Bereits in der Arbeitsanweisung erfährst du, ob du ganze Sätze schreiben sollst oder ob Kurzantworten/Einzelwörter ausreichen. Lies also die Aufgabenstellung aufmerksam durch. Meist reichen bei dieser „Writing"-Aufgabe Stichpunkte aus.

E-Mail/Brief/Nachricht

Hier musst du entweder ein offizielles Schreiben verfassen oder eine persönliche E-Mail, einen persönlichen Brief bzw. eine Nachricht über eine „messaging app" auf deinem Smartphone schreiben. Sieh dir die Aufgabenstellung genau an und analysiere im ersten Schritt, an wen sich dein Text richtet: Sollst du eine förmliche Anfrage, z. B. an eine Firma, oder eine persönliche Nachricht an Freunde oder Verwandte formulieren? Oft musst du als „fiktive", also erfundene Person einem fiktiven Adressaten schreiben. In welchem Stil dein Text geschrieben sein sollte, hängt von all diesen Faktoren ab.

- **Formelle(r) E-Mail/Brief:** Typische Beispiele für formelle E-Mails und Briefe sind Bewerbungen auf eine Stellenanzeige oder Kundenbeschwerden bzw. -anfragen. Bei dieser Art von Schreiben ist es wichtig, einen eher sachlichen Sprachstil zu verwenden. Vermeide Kurzformen wie „you're" oder „I'd" und verwende stattdessen die Langformen (also z. B. „you are" und „I would"). Achte auch auf eine passende Anfangs- und Schlussformel. Welche Wendungen sich hierfür eignen, erfährst du in Kapitel 4.2 – dort findest du auch weitere nützliche Formulierungshilfen.
- **Persönliche(r) E-Mail/Brief:** Bei einer persönlichen E-Mail oder einem persönlichen Brief an einen Freund oder eine Freundin kann dein Tonfall ruhig etwas lockerer sein – auch Kurzformen oder eher umgangssprachliche Ausdrücke sind erlaubt. Oft ist in der Aufgabenstellung bereits eine E-Mail vorgegeben, auf die du reagieren sollst. Lies dir den Text dann genau durch und versuche, auf die Aussagen oder Fragen darin einzugehen und deinen Text so zu formulieren, dass er zum Tonfall der vorgegebenen E-Mail passt.
- **Persönliche Nachricht:** Oftmals wird von dir verlangt, dass du eine knappe „message" formulierst. In deiner Abschlussprüfung wird in der Regel eine Situation in der Arbeitsanweisung vorgegeben, auf die du reagieren sollst. Manchmal enthält die Aufgabenstellung auch ein Bild, auf das du Bezug nehmen sollst. Auch hier solltest du an die Anrede zu Beginn denken und am Ende (d)einen Namen ergänzen.

Artikel

Häufig sollst du in der Abschlussprüfung einen Artikel schreiben. Es kann sich dabei z. B. um einen Beitrag für eine englischsprachige Schülerzeitung oder für eine Jugendzeitschrift handeln, in dem du eine bestimmte Fragestellung bzw. Problematik besprichst und ggf. dazu Stellung nimmst. Manchmal sollst du auch einen Artikel für einen Schreibwettbewerb verfassen. Achte auch hier wieder darauf, was genau von dir verlangt wird. Artikel für die Schülerzeitung sollten sachlich, aber trotzdem lebendig geschrieben sein; bei einem Beitrag für einen offiziellen Wettbewerb kann ein eher förmlicher Stil erforderlich sein, usw.

Geschichte

Auch das Verfassen einer Geschichte ist eine beliebte Aufgabenstellung. Hier gibt es viele verschiedene Möglichkeiten, wie die Aufgabe gestaltet sein kann. Vielleicht ist dir ein **Bild** vorgegeben und du sollst dazu eine Geschichte erfinden, vielleicht liegt dir aber auch der **Anfang einer Geschichte** vor und du sollst die „story" (mithilfe von weiteren Vorgaben) zu Ende führen. Besonders bei dieser Textsorte ist es wichtig, den Spannungsbogen aufrechtzuerhalten und den Leser oder die Leserin „bei der Stange zu halten". Dies funktioniert in der Regel nur, wenn du dir vor dem Schreiben die Zeit nimmst und eine ausführliche Ideensammlung machst. Wichtig ist auch, dass du dir klar machst, aus welcher Perspektive die Geschichte erzählt werden soll. Manchmal ist die Perspektive vorgegeben, aber gelegentlich kannst du auch frei entscheiden, ob du als Ich-Erzähler auftreten willst oder ob die „story" in der 3. Person erzählt werden soll.

Tagebuch- oder Blogeintrag

Manchmal wird auch von dir verlangt, über bestimmte Erfahrungen oder Erlebnisse zu berichten, z. B. in Form eines Tagebuch- oder Blogeintrags. Diese Texte sind oft in einem eher informellen, lockeren Stil gehalten. Sie sind in der 1. Person Singular verfasst und greifen meist ein besonderes oder einschneidendes Erlebnis auf, d. h., es bietet sich häufig an, auch auf Gefühle einzugehen.

In Kapitel 4.4 hast du Gelegenheit, einige der typischen Aufgabenformate der Abschlussprüfung gezielt zu trainieren. Darüber hinaus enthält das Kapitel zu Beginn auch mehrere vorbereitende Übungen, mit denen du dich langsam an das Schreiben längerer Texte herantasten kannst.

4.4 Übungsaufgaben zum Bereich „Writing"

1. **Gap sentences**
   Fill in the correct conjunctions:

when – while – in order to – because – but

a) I took an umbrella with me this morning ________________ it was raining.

b) __________ I'm 18 years old I will leave home.

c) I'd love to visit New York, __________ I don't have enough money.

d) Jack moved to another town ________________ become independent.

e) Clara washes the dishes _____________ she's talking to her best friend on the phone.

2. **Gap sentences**
   Fill in an appropriate expression *(einen passenden Ausdruck)* from the following list to complete the text.

but – In my opinion – and – Secondly – but all in all I believe that – Another aspect is that – First of all – In addition to that – you could argue that

Hi, my name is Amy, I am 16 years old and I love watching talent shows such as "The Voice". ____________________________, talent shows are great. __________________, they give people the chance to show their musical talent to a big audience. ___________________, these shows can also give them the chance to earn money with their music. ____________________ some young people are not very self-confident, _____________ when they are given the opportunity to be on stage and to get applause, their self-confidence can grow.

______________________, people who make it to the finals get a lot of tips on how to find their own style. Of course, ____________________________ the fame and the money don't make anyone happy _____________ that these shows are too much stress for young people, ___________________________________ talent shows help the participants to develop their musical talents.

3. Choose the **correct beginning** for each situation.

   a) In a letter to Carlos Fernandez, your pen friend in South America:
      - ☐ Dear Mr Fernandez,
      - ☐ Sir,
      - ☐ Hi Carlos,

   b) In an e-mail to Diana Watson, the manager of a hotel you stayed at (you only know her name and have never met her in person):
      - ☐ Dear Ms Watson,
      - ☐ Dear Mrs Watson,
      - ☐ Dear Sir / Madam,

   c) In a letter of application to the personnel manager of a company:
      - ☐ Dear lady or gentleman,
      - ☐ Dear Sir or Madam,
      - ☐ Dear everyone,

   d) In an e-mail to Linda Evans, your grandmother:
      - ☐ Dear Granny,
      - ☐ Hi Evans,
      - ☐ Dear Mrs Evans,

4. Choose the **correct ending** for each situation.

   a) In a letter to Carlos Fernandez, Mike's new pen friend in South America:
      - ☐ Love, Mike
      - ☐ Best wishes, Mike
      - ☐ Yours sincerely, Mike

   b) In an e-mail to Diana Watson, the manager of a hotel you stayed at (you only know her name and have never met her in person):
      - ☐ Yours sincerely,
      - ☐ Love,
      - ☐ Best wishes,

   c) In a letter of application to the personnel manager of a company:
      - ☐ Regards,
      - ☐ Yours faithfully,
      - ☐ All the best,

   d) In an e-mail to Linda Evans, your grandmother:
      - ☐ Yours sincerely,
      - ☐ Yours faithfully,
      - ☐ Love,

5. **A form** – Your student magazine is doing a survey among the pupils at your school. Fill in the form below.

What year are you in?	☐ 5 ☐ 6 ☐ 7 ☐ 8 ☐ 9 ☐ 10
How do you get to school?	
How long does it take you to get to school?	
What is your favourite subject?	
What do you like about our school? Name two things.	• ________ • ________
What do you not like about our school? Name two things.	• ________ • ________
What do you think about the technical equipment?	
What do you think about the sports facilities (gym, sports field)?	

6. **A form** – You are on holiday in Greece. In Athens you meet someone from the National Tourist Board, who tells you that if you fill in the questionnaire on Greece, you can win a one-week holiday for two in a luxury hotel not far from Athens. Of course you fill in the form:

FULL NAME:	
HOME ADDRESS:	
E-MAIL:	
AGE:	
SEX:	NATIONALITY:
How did you get to Greece?	
Where are you staying?	
How long are you staying in Greece?	
What do you like best about Greece?	
Could you also imagine travelling to Greece in winter? Why? / Why not?	

THANK YOU FOR TAKING PART IN OUR SURVEY!

7. **A note** – Imagine you are visiting your Scottish aunt. Your aunt works at the local hospital and today her shift ends around noon. As she is always hungry when she gets home, you have prepared something for her to eat. However, you won't be home when she gets there, so you write her a note in about **50 words**.

In your note, tell her …
- where you have gone and with who,
- when you will be back,
- what you have prepared for her.

8. **An application** – Your aunt Sarah lives in England. You are staying with her in the summer holidays. As you would like to earn some money and improve your English you apply for the following job. Write about **80 words**.

Help needed!

Summer job at Charles' Cleaners in Springdale

Small family business requires help in dry cleaning shop. Sort laundry (before and after cleaning), serve customers. No contact with chemicals. Friendly teenager welcome.

Send application to:
springdale@cleaners.co.uk

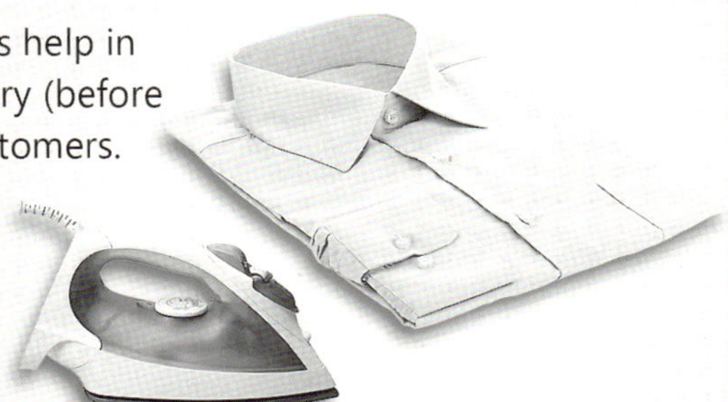

Write about …
- yourself.
- your qualifications.
- why you would be suited for the job.

9. **A discussion board entry** – On an internet forum you find the following discussion: "Should teenagers be allowed to vote at the age of 16?"
Write a text of about **80 words**. Write about …
- pros.
- cons.
- your own opinion.

10. **A message – The lost guidebook**
You are visiting a friend in the north of England. You have gone to London for the weekend, but your friend couldn't go with you. He lent you his London guidebook. Unfortunately, you cannot find it anymore.
Send your friend a message.

In your text,
- apologise,
- explain why you lost the guidebook,
- tell your friend what you would like to do to make up for it.

Write about **100 words**.

11. **A formal message** – You see an advertisement for a holiday in Britain on-line and you want some more information.

Treat yourself to a city break!

London – Birmingham – Liverpool – Edinburgh – Glasgow – Cardiff

From £ 50 per night

- 3-star or 4-star hotels
- breakfast included
- a place for everyone: single, double or family rooms
- optional: sightseeing tour package
- airport shuttle possible
- ticket service

Any questions? Just get in touch –
Write an email to info@citybreak.co.uk **or use our** **contact** form

Use the contact form below to write a formal message in about **100 words**.

In your message …

- mention which city you have chosen.
- say when you would like to go and what type of room you need.
- ask about the prices, hotel locations and facilities (e. g. gym, spa, Wi-Fi).

Contact us

Name

Email

Subject

Your message

Send

12. **A story about a picture – Bullying?**

a) Take a close look at the picture. Think of four more questions you could ask about it.

- Why is the boy sad?
-
-
-
-

b) Imagine what is going on between the boy in the foreground and the other teenagers. Think of answers to the questions you asked in task a) and write a short story in about **120 words**.

13. **A personal e-mail – A language course in San Francisco**

In the summer holidays, you are going to attend a language course in San Francisco. You are travelling together with an Italian friend you met on your last holiday.

Here's your friend's e-mail:

Hi there,

So cool – only a few more weeks and we'll be in San Francisco together!
OK, we've got English lessons in the morning, but we'll have plenty of time to explore the city, too. Have you got any special plans? I've attached two nice pictures to give you some ideas ☺.
Did you also get an e-mail from the language school today? They want to know whether we would like to stay with a host family or share an apartment with other students from the language course.
What do you think? I think it would be fun if we could stay at the same place.

Best wishes,
Fabio

Write an answer to Fabio. In your e-mail, include the following aspects:

- at least one activity you would like to do in San Francisco
- advantages of sharing an apartment with other students and/or of staying in a host family
- which of the two options you would prefer and why

Find a suitable beginning and ending. Write about **120 words**.

a) Make a table and **collect ideas** for your e-mail.

b) Write the e-mail to Fabio.

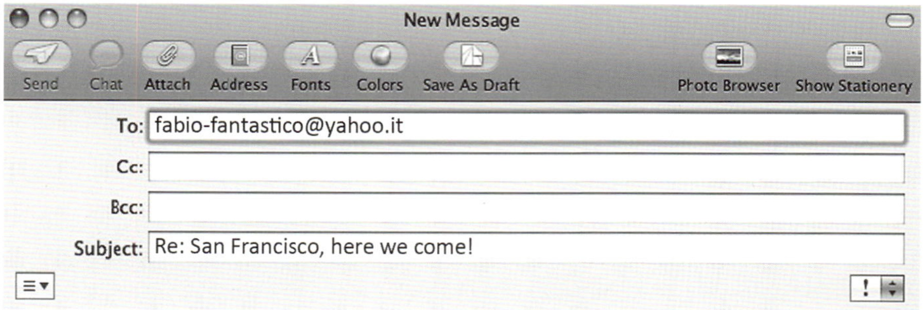

14. **A story – My first day on planet Earth**

Think about who is telling the story. Finish the story in **120–150 words** and write about …

- what X23 experiences / experienced on Earth,
- what he / she / it finds / found strange,
- a surprising or funny ending.

Hi, I'm X23 and it's my first day on planet Earth. …

15. **An article – No social networks for a week**
For a school project you and your classmates have decided to live without social networks for one week. Write an article for your English school magazine about your experiences during this week.

Include the following aspects:
- the initial idea for the project
- advantages and disadvantages of social networks
- what you learnt from the experience

Write about **150 words**.

16. **A formal e-mail/complaint – A holiday nightmare**

You are back from a holiday in Britain. Unfortunately, your accommodation turned out to be a real nightmare.

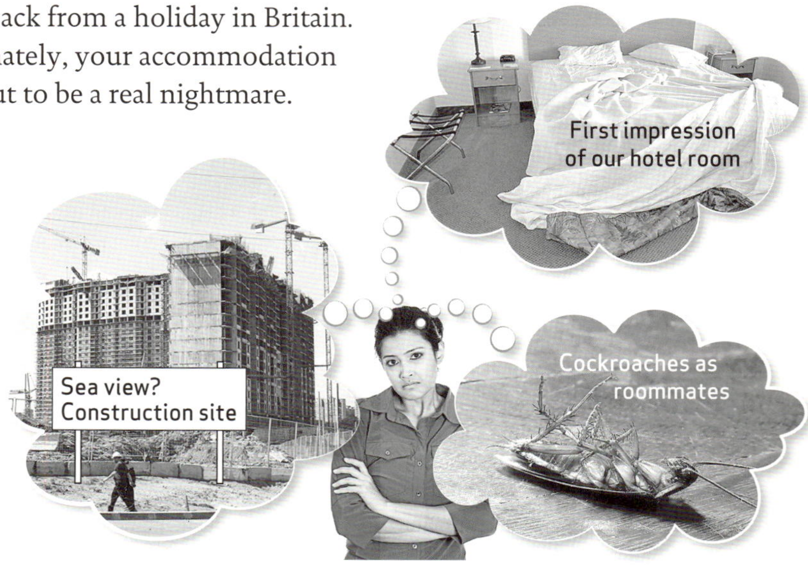

Write an e-mail and complain to the English travel agency. Write about **150 words**.

Include the following aspects:

- the promises made on the agency's website
- what the hotel was like in reality
- what you expect the company to do next

Find a suitable beginning and ending.

5 Speaking

Immer wieder wird im Unterricht deine mündliche Kommunikationsfähigkeit überprüft. Auch im Rahmen der Abschlussprüfung gibt es einen mündlichen Prüfungsteil. Das sogenannte „oral exam" findet ein paar Wochen vor der schriftlichen Prüfung statt; die mündliche Note fließt mit einem Drittel in das Gesamtergebnis der Abschlussprüfung ein.

5.1 Strategien zum Bereich „Speaking"

Langfristige Vorbereitung

Sich in einer Fremdsprache mündlich auszudrücken, ist nicht einfach. Man kann sich auch nicht kurzfristig – quasi über Nacht – auf diesen Prüfungsbereich vorbereiten. Will man in einer mündlichen Prüfung gut abschneiden, dann muss man **langfristig** und **nachhaltig** an der Sprechfertigkeit arbeiten.
Übungsmöglichkeiten bietet dir dein Englischunterricht. Nimm aktiv am Unterrichtsgeschehen teil, d. h., melde dich so oft wie möglich und sprich auf Englisch. So gewinnst du mit der Zeit Routine und wirst nach und nach gelassener. Wenn du dabei künftig auch noch die folgenden grundsätzlichen Tipps und Hinweise berücksichtigst, klappt das mit der Zeit sicherlich recht gut.

TIPP

- Nutze die Übungsphasen im Unterricht.
- Sprich deutlich und nicht zu schnell.
- Frage nach, wenn du etwas nicht verstanden hast.
- Vermeide einfache, kurze Antworten wie „yes" oder „no". Mit solchen Antworten kannst du keine Gespräche in Gang halten und auch deine mündliche Ausdrucksfähigkeit nicht unter Beweis stellen. Wenn es passend ist, begründe deine Meinung oder füge ein Beispiel an.
- Wenn du unsicher oder nervös bist, bilde lieber kürzere Sätze.
- Lerne die hilfreichen Wendungen (siehe 5.4) auswendig und wende sie immer wieder an. Auf diese Weise werden sie Teil deines aktiven Wortschatzes und es wird dir leichtfallen, sie auch in der mündlichen Prüfung zu benutzen.
- Bemühe dich, Sachverhalte auf unterschiedliche Weise auszudrücken, um zu zeigen, dass du einen vielfältigen Wortschatz hast. Beschränke dich also z. B. nicht auf „I think", um deine Meinung auszudrücken.
- Versuche, dich auch in deiner Freizeit mit der englischen Sprache zu beschäftigen. Du kannst z. B. englische Zeitschriften oder Bücher lesen, Fernsehsendungen oder Filme auf Englisch ansehen, ein Tagebuch auf Englisch führen oder die Grundeinstellung deines Handys auf die Fremdsprache ändern. Auf diese Weise wirst du immer vertrauter und sicherer im Gebrauch des Englischen.

5.2 Das „oral exam“

Ablauf der Prüfung

- Es werden immer zwei oder (in Ausnahmefällen) drei Schüler*innen gleichzeitig geprüft. Wer mit wem zusammen geprüft wird, wird per Los entschieden. Du brauchst aber keine Angst zu haben, denn auch wenn dein Partner oder deine Partnerin vielleicht nicht so gut Englisch spricht, kannst du trotzdem die volle Punktzahl bekommen, denn deine Leistung wird unabhängig von der der anderen Prüflinge bewertet.
- Es sind immer zwei Lehrkräfte dabei. In der Regel sind das dein Englischlehrer bzw. deine Englischlehrerin und noch eine zweite Fachlehrkraft, die das Protokoll schreibt. Dein Lehrer oder deine Lehrerin führt das Prüfungsgespräch.
- Das „oral exam“ für den G-Kurs dauert in etwa 10–12 Minuten.
  Für den E-Kurs sind rund 12–15 Minuten angesetzt.

Aufbau der Prüfung

Beachte, dass zwar die Bestandteile der Prüfung vom Ministerium festgelegt sind, dass jedoch die genaue Ausarbeitung der Prüfung an deiner Schule stattfindet. Höre also genau zu, wenn du im Unterricht wichtige Informationen zur Prüfung erhältst.
Das „oral exam“ besteht aus drei Teilen mit jeweils verschiedenen Aufgabenstellungen:

- **G-Kurs**
  - Speaking about yourself
  - Information gap activity
  - Speaking prompts
- **E-Kurs**
  - Speaking about yourself
  - Speaking prompts
  - Paired / Group discussion

5.3 Prüfungsteile des „oral exam“

G-Kurs und E-Kurs: Part I

Speaking about yourself

Die Prüfung beginnt mit einer kurzen Begrüßung und Vorstellung der zweiten Lehrkraft. Häufig folgt dann die Frage, wie es dir geht. Danach werden dir Fragen gestellt, bei denen du etwas über dich selbst bzw. deine Lebensumstände erzählen kannst. Es kann sein, dass du z. B. auch deinen Namen oder deine Straße buchstabieren musst. Wiederhole also unbedingt noch einmal das Buchstabieren.

Die Fragen können im Allgemeinen vier Bereichen zugeordnet werden:
- *my family*
- *my city/village*
- *my hobbies/my free-time/activities*
- *my school/my class/my course/my career*

TIPP

Diesen Teil kannst du schon langfristig vor der Prüfung vorbereiten und intensiv üben, indem du dir Aussagen zu deiner Familie, deinem Wohnort, deinen Hobbys etc. überlegst. Bereite z. B. Mindmaps vor, in denen du verschiedene Aspekte notierst. Du kannst sie im Laufe der Zeit immer wieder ergänzen. Übe regelmäßig und am besten mit jemandem, der dir Rückmeldung geben und dich verbessern kann. Dadurch, dass du dir nur Stichpunkte notierst, bleibst du sprachlich flexibler und kannst in der mündlichen Prüfung besser auf die Fragen, die dir gestellt werden, reagieren.

Information gap activity

G-Kurs: Part II

Hier wird dir und deinem Mitprüfling eine bestimmte Situation anhand von Stichpunkten vorgestellt, in die ihr euch hineinversetzen müsst. Beachtet, dass auf euren Rollenkarten unterschiedliche Informationen stehen. Ihr müsst euch nun miteinander unterhalten und gemäß euren Rollenvorgaben Informationen austauschen. Wichtig ist, dass ihr jeweils auf die Äußerungen der anderen Person eingeht, sodass ein echter Dialog entsteht.

TIPP

- Übe immer wieder mit verschiedenen Mitschülerinnen und Mitschülern.
- Sieh dir das ausgehändigte Material in Ruhe an und nimm dir die Zeit, die Vorgaben genau durchzulesen.
- Höre deinem Gegenüber aufmerksam zu. Wenn du eine Aussage oder Frage nicht verstanden hast, traue dich nachzufragen. Nur so kannst du angemessen auf den Redebeitrag der anderen Person reagieren.

Speaking prompts

G-Kurs: Part III
E-Kurs: Part II

Hier musst du in den meisten Fällen ein Bild bzw. Foto beschreiben und näher analysieren. Abschließend ist es deine Aufgabe, die dargestellte Situation auf dich selbst zu beziehen und z. B. über deine Vorlieben für und Abneigungen gegen die abgebildete Gegebenheit oder Aktivität (wie z. B. eine bestimmte Sportart) zu sprechen. Du kannst alles sagen, was dir zu deinem Bild einfällt. Wichtig ist, dass du englisch sprichst. Kleinere Grammatikfehler sind nicht so gravierend. Du kannst trotz einiger Grammatikfehler immer noch die volle Punktzahl erhalten. Entscheidend ist, dass der Inhalt deiner Äußerungen verständlich ist. Du sollst in etwa zwei Minuten über das Bild sprechen. Danach können sich Fragen anschließen, die du beantworten musst.

TIPP

Sieh dir das Material (z. B. Foto) genau an und beschreibe es im Detail. Nutze die dir zur Verfügung stehende Zeit und sage alles, was dir dazu einfällt. Du brauchst keine Panik zu bekommen, wenn dir ein wichtiges Wort fehlt. Konzentriere dich dann einfach bei deiner Beschreibung auf andere Aspekte.

Folgende Fragen können dir bei einer Bildbeschreibung helfen, deine Antwort zu strukturieren:
- *What is happening?*
  Denk daran, das *present progressive* zu verwenden, wenn du beschreibst, was auf einem Bild gerade passiert.
- *How many people are in the picture? How old are they? Where are they? What do they look like? What are they wearing? What is their relationship to each other?*
- *When or where was the photo taken? Why are these people in this place?*
- *What is the main theme or message?*
- *What else can you say about it?*
- *What do you think about the picture? Why do / don't you like it? …*

E-Kurs: Part III

Paired / Group discussion

Hier wird dir und dem anderen Prüfling (bzw. den anderen Prüflingen) eine bestimmte Situation anhand von Stichpunkten und / oder Bildmaterial vorgestellt, in die ihr euch hineinversetzen müsst. Ihr sollt euch nun miteinander unterhalten, Informationen austauschen und eure Meinungen und Gefühle ausdrücken. Je nach Situation sollt ihr am Ende zu einer Entscheidung gelangen. Wichtig ist, dass ihr gegenseitig auf eure Äußerungen eingeht, sodass ein echter Dialog entsteht. Rückfragen eignen sich hierfür auch sehr gut. Insgesamt soll ein richtiges Gespräch entstehen, d. h., ihr könnt nicht einfach etwas sagen, das nicht zum vorangegangenen Redebeitrag passt.

TIPP

- Übe immer wieder mit verschiedenen Mitschüler*innen.
- Sieh dir das ausgehändigte Material in Ruhe an und nimm dir die Zeit, die Vorgaben genau durchzulesen.
- Höre im Gespräch aufmerksam zu. Wenn du eine Aussage oder Frage nicht verstanden hast, traue dich nachzufragen. Nur so kannst du angemessen auf Redebeiträge anderer reagieren.

5.4 Hilfreiche Wendungen

Die folgenden Wörter und Ausdrücke helfen dir in Gesprächen. Du solltest sie auswendig lernen. Die Wendungen sind übrigens auch als digitale „MindCards" verfügbar, mit denen du am Smartphone oder Tablet üben kannst.

Speaking

Bildbeschreibung *(Describing pictures)*

In the picture I / we can see …	*In dem Bild kann ich/können wir … sehen.*
The photo shows …	*Das Foto zeigt …*
It was taken in …	*Es wurde in … aufgenommen.*
In the background / foreground there is / there are …	*Im Hintergrund/Vordergrund ist/ sind …*
In the centre / middle of the picture …	*Im Bildmittelpunkt …*
On the left / right of the photo …	*Links/Rechts im Foto …*
The person in the top left-hand / bottom right-hand corner …	*Die Person in der linken oberen/ rechten unteren Ecke …*
At the top / bottom you can see …	*Oben/Unten kann man … sehen.*
Next to / Near …	*Neben/In der Nähe …*
Behind / In front of …	*Hinter/Vor …*
On top of / Under …	*Auf/Unter …*
Between … and …	*Zwischen … und …*

Mit folgenden Ausdrücken kannst du Vermutungen anstellen und deine Meinung über das Bild ausdrücken:

It seems as if …	*Es scheint, als ob …*
The boy seems to …	*Der Junge scheint zu …*
Maybe …	*Vielleicht …*
The atmosphere is happy / sad / …	*Die Stimmung ist glücklich/ traurig …*
I (don't) like the photo, because …	*Ich mag das Foto (nicht), weil …*
The photo makes me think of / reminds me of …	*Das Foto erinnert mich an …*

Eine eigene Meinung ausdrücken *(Expressing an opinion)*

I (don't) think / believe / expect / imagine / suppose (that) …	*Ich glaube (nicht), (dass) …*
In my opinion / view …	*Meiner Meinung nach …*
That's not my opinion.	*Das ist nicht meine Meinung.*
I'm (not) sure / certain …	*Ich bin (nicht) sicher …*
I (don't) doubt (that) …	*Ich bezweifle (nicht), (dass) …*

I would / wouldn't …	*Ich würde (nicht) …*
I would like / I'd like …	*Ich würde / möchte gern …*
I don't like / I dislike …	*Ich mag … nicht.*
I would / wouldn't prefer …	*Ich würde lieber / würde lieber nicht …*
I'm for …	*Ich bin für … / dafür, dass …*
I'm against …	*Ich bin gegen … / dagegen, dass …*

Andere nach ihrer Meinung fragen (*Asking other people for an opinion*)

What do you think about … ?	*Was denkst du über … ?*
What's your opinion on / view on / reaction to … ?	*Was ist deine Meinung zu … ? / Was denkst du über … ?*
How do you see / view the situation / this?	*Wie siehst du die Situation / das?*
What would you say about … ?	*Was würdest du über / zum Thema … sagen?*
How do you (personally) feel about … ?	*Was hältst du (persönlich) von … ?*
Could you explain something to me?	*Könntest du mir etwas erklären?*
What about (the prohibition of drinking alcohol in public places)? Do you think that's right?	*Was denkst du über (das Verbot, Alkohol in der Öffentlichkeit zu trinken)? Glaubst du, dass das richtig / in Ordnung ist?*
I don't suppose you'll agree, will you? / … you would agree, would you? *(eine Antwort fordernd)*	*Du wirst sicher nicht zustimmen, oder?*

Du kannst auch Fragen mit Verneinungen stellen, um dein Gegenüber zu einer Meinungsäußerung zu bringen:

Don't you think that … ?	*Glaubst du nicht, dass … ?*
Wouldn't you like to see … ?	*Hättest du nicht auch lieber … ?*
Shouldn't we … ?	*Sollten wir nicht … ?*

Zustimmen und widersprechen (*Agreeing and disagreeing*)

This is / That's true.	*Das stimmt.*
I agree (with you).	*Ich bin deiner Meinung.*
(I'm sorry but) I disagree (with you).	*Ich bin nicht deiner Meinung.*
Yes, of course.	*Ja, natürlich.*
No, not at all.	*Nein, ganz und gar nicht.*
That's a good / great / fantastic idea.	*Das ist ein guter / großartiger / fantastischer Vorschlag.*

Excuse me but I think that's a bad idea. / That's a bad idea.	*Das ist keine gute Idee.*
You're right (about / that ...).	*Du hast recht (mit/wenn du sagst, dass ...).*
I'm sorry, but you're wrong (about ... / about that).	*Das stimmt nicht.*

Wenn du entsprechende Adverbien vor „right“, „wrong“ und „understand“ stellst, wird deine Antwort sehr deutlich.

You're absolutely right.	*Du hast völlig recht.*
You're totally wrong.	*Du liegst völlig falsch.*
I think you don't really understand (the problem).	*Ich glaube, du verstehst (das Problem) überhaupt nicht.*

Wenn du dir mit deiner Meinung nicht sicher bist, verwende Ausdrücke wie:

I'm not sure / certain.	*Ich bin (mir) nicht sicher.*

Jemanden unterbrechen *(Interrupting someone)*

Can I ask you something?	*Kann ich dich etwas fragen?*
Can / May I (just) say something, please?	*Kann ich bitte etwas sagen?*
Excuse me, but ...	*Entschuldigung, aber ...*
I don't wish to stop you but / I'm sorry to interrupt but ...	*Ich möchte dich nicht unterbrechen, aber ... / Ich unterbreche dich ungern, aber ...*
I'm sorry, I don't agree with ...	*Ich bin anderer Meinung (als) ...*
I'm sorry, that's not right / fair.	*Das ist nicht richtig/fair.*
I'm sorry, but (I'd just like to say) ...	*Es tut mir leid, aber (ich möchte kurz anmerken) ...*
You're wrong there. *(nachdrücklich)*	*Du hast nicht recht./Da hast du mit Sicherheit nicht recht.*
I don't think you're right.	*Ich glaube, dass du nicht recht hast.*
Oh, come on! You don't really believe that. *(wütend)*	*Das glaubst du doch selber nicht.*
How can you say that?	*Wie kannst du das sagen?*

Darum bitten, dass etwas wiederholt wird *(Asking for something to be repeated)*

Excuse me, could you say that again, please?	*Kannst du das bitte noch einmal sagen?*
Sorry, could you repeat that / what you said about ... ?	*Kannst du das bitte wiederholen?*

I'm sorry / I'm afraid I didn't quite hear / catch / understand what you said. Could you say it again / repeat it, please?	*Es tut mir leid, aber ich habe nicht genau verstanden, was du meinst/ gesagt hast. Kannst du das bitte noch einmal sagen?*
I'm sorry / I'm afraid, I missed / forgot what you were saying (about ...). Could you explain it again / once more, please?	*Es tut mir leid, ich habe nicht verstanden/ich habe vergessen, was du (über ...) gesagt hast. Kannst du das bitte noch einmal erklären?*
I'm sorry / I'm afraid, you were talking a bit too fast for me – could you say it again a little bit more slowly / would you mind repeating what you said, please?	*Es tut mir leid, du hast für mich etwas zu schnell gesprochen. Könntest du das bitte etwas langsamer wiederholen?*

Ein bereits behandeltes Thema aufgreifen *(Returning to an earlier topic)*

You said earlier ...	*Du hast vorhin gesagt ...*
You mentioned / talked about ...	*Du hast ... erwähnt.*
A few minutes ago you said ...	*Vor ein paar Minuten hast du gesagt ...*
As you said before ...	*Wie du vorhin/schon gesagt hast, ...*
Can we go back to ... for a minute?	*Können wir noch einmal auf ... zurückkommen?*

Das Thema wechseln *(Changing the subject)*

We've talked a lot about ... Could we look at ... now?	*Wir haben viel über ... geredet. Könnten wir jetzt über ... sprechen?*
Can we move on and talk about ... ?	*Können wir weitermachen und über ... reden?*
We should really talk about ... too.	*Wir sollten wirklich auch über ... reden.*
That's my opinion about (tennis). But what about (football)? What do you think about it?	*So denke ich über (Tennis). Aber was meinst du zu (Fußball)/hältst du von (Fußball)?*
Can we talk about ... now?	*Können wir jetzt über ... sprechen?*
Perhaps we should also talk about ...	*Vielleicht sollten wir auch über ... reden.*
Can / May I say something at this point?	*Kann ich an dieser Stelle etwas sagen?*

Andere zum Reden bringen (*Making people talk*)

Direkte Fragen mit Fragewörtern wie „what", „why", „where", „when", „who", „which", „how":

What do you think, (Anne)?	*Was meinst du, (Anne)?*
Why do / don't you think so?	*Warum glaubst du das (nicht)?*
Can we find a solution together?	*Können wir zusammen eine Lösung finden?*

Entscheidungsfragen:

Are you interested in … ?	*Interessierst du dich für … ?*
Do you want … ?	*Willst du … ?*

Bestätigungsfragen:

The weather is terrible today, isn't it?	*Das Wetter ist schrecklich, oder?*
It isn't cold outside, is it?	*Es ist nicht kalt draußen, oder?*

TIPP

Manchmal musst du kurz überlegen, bis du weißt, was du sagen möchtest. Damit das Gespräch dennoch nicht unterbrochen wird, kannst du folgende Füllwörter benutzen:

- *Well, …*
- *Let me see … / I see …*
- *I'm not sure, but …*
- *What I'm trying to say is …*
- *Actually, I think …*
- *I guess …*

Lerne diese Ausdrücke auswendig und versuche, sie bereits während des Unterrichts im Gespräch anzuwenden.

Wenn einer von euch nicht mehr weiter weiß, kann der andere mit solchen Fragen helfen:

- *Are you saying that …?*
- *What do you think about … ? / Don't you think that … ?*

5.5 Übungsaufgaben zum Bereich „Speaking“

Speaking about yourself

Hinweis *In diesem Prüfungsteil musst du Fragen zu dir und deiner Lebenssituation beantworten. In der folgenden Übung sollst du in Vorbereitung auf mögliche Prüfungsfragen eine Mindmap erstellen.*

1. Make a mind map of your family. The following aspects might help you. Feel free to add other details, too.
   - your family members' names
   - their ages
   - your parents' jobs
   - your family members' hobbies
   - your house / your flat
   - the activities you do together
   - where you have gone on holiday / are planning to go on holiday
   - what you like / don't like about your family
   - your grandparents / aunts / uncles …
   - your pet
   - …

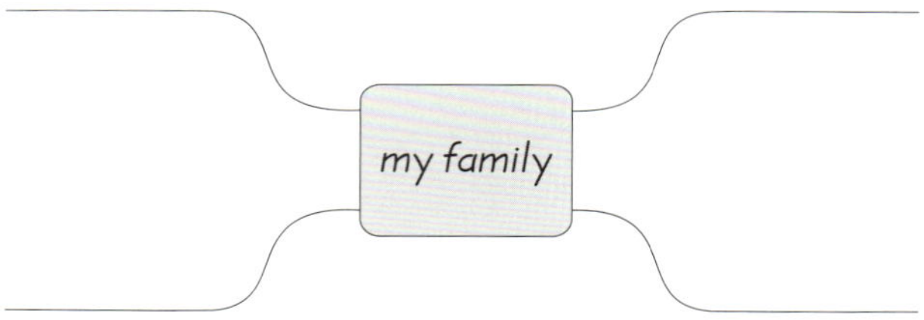

Hinweis *Versuche, in einem zweiten Schritt mithilfe deiner Mindmap eine zusammenhängende und gut strukturierte Antwort auf die Frage deines Lehrers oder deiner Lehrerin zu geben.*

2. **Teacher:** Tell me something about your family.
   You: Well, in my family, there are …

Information gap activity

In diesem Teil der mündlichen Prüfung führst du mit deinem Mitschüler/deiner Mitschülerin ein Gespräch zu einem vorgegebenen Thema. Es kann sein, dass ihr Rollenkarten bekommt, die unterschiedliche Informationen enthalten. Die Stichpunkte auf euren Rollenkarten führen euch als roter Faden durch das Gespräch. Dabei kann es sich z. B. um ein Verkaufsgespräch im Supermarkt oder an der Kinokasse, um ein Gespräch mit einem Austauschschüler/einer Austauschschülerin oder um die Organisation einer Party/Schulveranstaltung handeln.

Hinweis

3. "At the cinema"

Teacher: In this part of the test you are going to talk to each other. One of you wants to buy cinema tickets, the other one works at the ticket office. When you have read your prompts, you can start with your dialogue.

Rollenkarte A

You are on a trip through Great Britain and want to go to a cinema. You go to the ticket office to buy tickets for yourself and two of your friends. It is now 6.30 p.m.

Here are some prompts you can use:
- tickets for "The Royal Family"?
- number of tickets: 3
- time film ends?
- where to buy popcorn, something to drink?

Rollenkarte B

You sell tickets at the cinema in Birmingham. You are talking to the customer. It is now 6.30 p.m.

Here are some prompts you can use:
- how many tickets?
- £6 back rows, £4 front rows
- student ID? Ticket £1 cheaper
- end: 8.45 p.m.
- interested in film poster? → cinema shop

Speaking prompts

Hinweis

Sieh dir das Bild genau an und achte auf Details. Beschreibe, was du auf dem Bild siehst, und äußere dann ein paar persönliche Gedanken. Sag alles über das Bild, was dir einfällt. Wenn du jedoch ins Stocken gerätst, wird dir dein Lehrer oder deine Lehrerin Fragen stellen, die dir helfen, deine Redezeit zu nutzen.

4. **Teacher (to Candidate A):** Describe the picture, please.

Hinweis

Die Fragen, die sich an deine Bildbeschreibung anschließen können, hängen natürlich davon ab, auf welche Aspekte du bereits eingegangen bist. Mögliche „prompts" (Hilfestellungen) könnten z. B. sein:

Teacher:
- What has happened? / What will happen next?
- What could be the problem?
- Why are they sitting at the computer?

5. **Teacher (to Candidate B):** Describe the picture, please.

Possible prompts:

Teacher:
- What could the children be talking about?
- How is the girl feeling?
- What could happen next?
- Do you know anyone who has been in a situation like this?

Paired / Group discussion

In diesem Prüfungsteil führen die Prüflinge ein Gespräch zu einem vorgegebenen Thema. Häufig erhaltet ihr hierzu „visual prompts", also Bildimpulse, die die Grundlage eures Gesprächs bilden.

Hinweis

6. "Money for charity"

Teacher: At our summer party last year the school raised €2,500 to give to a charity. Which charity do you think we should give it to? Here are some we have selected, but of course you may have other ideas, too. Discuss carefully the reasons for and against each charity and try to come to a decision about what to do with the money.

6 Anhang: Hörverstehenstexte

Listening Test 1: Short conversations

Text 1 – Where does Tom want to go on holiday?

Jane: Where should we go on holiday this year, Tom?
Tom: I don't want to go to a city again. We went to one last year.
Jane: I'd like to go to Japan – we haven't been there yet.
Tom: I'm not sure I want to go there. I'd like to go somewhere different.
Jane: Like where? South Africa? Australia?
Tom: A safari in South Africa sounds fun. I'll see what's on the internet about it.

Text 2 – What does the man need?

Man: Excuse me, please. Can you help me?
Woman: Of course. Are you lost?
Man: No, I'm not. I just need some change for the ticket machine. It just takes coins or cards and I've only got a £ 5 note.
Woman: I'm sorry, I can't change that. Ask in the shop over there.
Man: Thank you, I'll do that.

Text 3 – How many minutes late is the train today?

Tina: I hate this train at the moment. Every day it arrives at a different time.
George: What time should it arrive?
Tina: At 6.33. But yesterday it was 10 minutes late, on Monday it was 13 minutes early and today it's 30 minutes late! Who knows when it will come tomorrow!
George: It's very annoying, isn't it?
Tina: Yes, it is, ... especially when you use it every day to get to work.

Text 4 – What did the bird take?

Phil: Hi, Julia. I'm going to Whitby tomorrow with my class.
Julia: That'll be fun.
Phil: Hope so, ... and I'm going to have some fish and chips and an ice cream.
Julia: Whitby has the best fish and chips in the world.
Phil: And the worst seagulls! Last year I was eating my fish and chips outside and one flew down and stole my fish! I only had my chips left!
Julia: A flying thief ... how cool is that!

Text 5 –Which question is difficult?

Teacher: Good morning everyone. So, how far did we get yesterday?
Sam: We'd just finished question 14 on page 40.
Teacher: That's right ... and today we're going to do questions 15 and 16.
Sam: Can I say something first?
Teacher: Of course, Sam, go on.

Sam: Most of us had a problem with number 14 ... I don't think anyone has got it right.

Teacher: Oh dear ... let's look at it again then before we do something new.

Text 6 – What is Emma going to buy?

Emma: I have to buy my little sister a birthday present. Any ideas?

Peter: Maybe she'll be happy with some pencils, felt pens and some paper.

Emma: That's not very much! What about some clothes? A T-shirt and a jumper maybe?

Peter: I don't know. What if they don't fit or she doesn't like them?

Emma: You're right. What about some paints and a book about painting then ... and some paper, of course.

Peter: She won't read a book about painting. Just get her what I suggested.

Emma: OK. Let's go into town.

Text 7 – Which way is lucky?

Annie: Simon ... help me!

Simon: What's wrong?

Annie: Cats. Black cats. We were talking in school about things people believe in – you know, superstitions and all that. And a black cat has just walked in front of me.

Simon: So?

Annie: So, if you see a black cat, does it bring you luck or not?

Simon: It can be both. In England, it's bad luck if it walks from right to left and good luck the other way. But, if it walks away from you, it's taking your luck with it – so that's really bad luck!

Listening Test 2: Short texts

Text 1 – Which group of people get onto the plane second?

Speaker: I'm pleased to tell you that flight TA 3654 to Toronto is now ready for boarding.

Unfortunately, we can only use the front door of the plane today, due to a faulty walkway to the rear one. This means that boarding will take a little longer than normal. Please listen carefully to the boarding procedure and have your boarding card and passport ready.

First class, business class and adults with small children may now start to board the plane. The next group of passengers to get on the plane are those in Economy – rows 25 to 35. Please look at your ticket to see which row you are seated in. Once these passengers have boarded, rows 10–24 may follow.

We would like to apologise for any inconvenience this may cause.

Text 2 – How will Daniel get home if his mum can't meet him?

Daniel: Oh … Hi, Mum … um … so, you're busy at work or doing something … OK, I'll leave a message. I'm still at Paddington Station – the train's late again. There's a bad storm near London and it's causing a lot of problems – trees blown down and things like that. I'll probably be in Exeter about 6.30 now – no guarantees about that, though, since there might be more disruption. Can you wait for me outside the station? If you can't make it, can you text me, please? I'll then get a taxi. It shouldn't be too expensive and it's quicker than the bus. See you later.

Text 3 – Which is the correct way to the hotel?

Tourist: Excuse me, I'm looking for the Castle Hotel.

Passer-by: Oh, I know where that is – it's in the marketplace.

Tourist: How do I get there?

Passer-by: Go straight ahead and turn left at the end of the road. Then … take the second road on your right. It'll take you straight to the marketplace. In the marketplace, go right. The hotel is about 50 metres further on your right but the entrance to it is just round the first corner.

Tourist: It sounds rather hard to find.

Passer-by: No, it's not – it just sounds difficult. You'll find it easily enough.

Tourist: Thank you.

Text 4 – What is Tom going to do now on Saturday?

Tom: Do you know what the weather is going to be like this weekend, Clara?

Clara: It isn't going to be great, Tom. There's heavy rain coming in from the Atlantic. The weather forecast on the radio also said it would be a wet start tomorrow for everyone. But in the South it should be sunny on Sunday.

Tom: Well, that's spoilt my plans. I was going to take the dogs for a long walk on the beach on Saturday but I won't bother now. They can have a quick run about in the park instead. What are you doing at the weekend?

Clara: I'm driving down to London on Saturday to see my sister. I'll be back on Monday.

Tom: So you'll have the nice weather on Sunday and me and my dogs will be getting very wet.

Clara: It looks that way, doesn't it?

Text 5 – Where will each group of friends wait?

Anna: Rosie's had a great idea for my birthday, Mum.

Mum: What's that?

Anna: Rosie said her dad would take us flying. His friend has got a four-seater plane he can fly and he'll take Rosie, me and four of our friends with him.

Mum: How's that going to work? That's six people.

Anna: He said that there's a small café at the airport where we can buy pizzas or sandwiches and sit outside to eat them. So he'll take three of us up in his plane for half an hour while the other three are eating. Then he'll land and we'll swap over.

Mum: That's really nice of him. How are you all going to get to the airport?

Anna: Mum's 7-seater taxi?

Text 6 – Where was Lilly when she found out that she'd lost her camera?

Harvey: Hi Lilly. How was your holiday?

Lilly: I had a great time but I lost my camera on the second day.

Harvey: That wasn't a very good start to your holiday. What happened?

Lilly: It was my own fault. I'd been walking around San Francisco for hours and saw a really nice bench. I sat down and after a while I saw a taxi – so I waved to it and the driver stopped. He took me back to my hotel. The next morning after breakfast I realised I'd left my camera on the bench!

Harvey: Didn't you go back for it?

Lilly: Do you really think it would still have been there? I don't.

Harvey: It might have.

Lilly: No way. But I had my smartphone with me so I could still take some holiday photos.

Listening Test 3: Sharks

Adam: Hi, Nicki. Nice to see you in the studio today.

Nicki: Thanks, Adam. It's great to be here.

Adam: So, one day you decided you'd fly to Florida and then jump in the sea with lots of hungry sharks?

Nicki: Not quite. I was in my last year at school and I wanted to do something different. Lots of my friends were talking about jobs and so on … and I was thinking: freedom, adventure, fun. Then one day I was surfing the internet looking for things I could do when I read about a group of people doing a study of sharks – shark research – and they wanted someone to help them.

Adam: Sharks aren't exactly friendly, are they? Weren't you worried about them?

Nicki: A little bit on the plane. But later I learnt so much about them. They've got a bad name, but that's not fair. They don't often attack people but when they do, it's often a mistake … and, apparently, people don't taste nice.

Adam: Oh, that's something!

Nicki: No, what I mean is sharks see people in wetsuits or on surfboards and they think: "Yummy, seal for dinner." So, if they're hungry they'll take a bite and then go, "Yuk, that's horrible!" There are usually just over 80 shark attacks every year in the whole world and only about five people are killed: dogs kill 25,000 people and crocodiles 1,000! Top of the table of bad guys are mosquitoes – actually did you know only the females bite? Anyway, … way down in 15th place is the poor shark.

Adam: Can you do anything to make the risk of a shark attack even less?

Nicki: Sure. Always go into clear water – then a shark can see if you're a seal or not. Don't go into the sea in the early morning or late evening – sharks like to hunt then. And if you can, stay close to other people – sharks don't like groups.

Adam: Interesting. Let's take a break and play some music and we'll be back with Nicki in a few minutes.

Listening Test 4: The California Gold Rush

Speaker: In 1847, California became a US territory. Most Americans at the time lived on the East Coast. But thousands traveled west to California after a settler reported finding gold there.

James Marshall found the gold nugget in January 1848. Mr Marshall was building a sawmill near the American River in central California. When he looked in the water, he saw shiny pieces of metal. One of them was about the size of a fingernail. Mr Marshall took the piece and put it in his mouth.

Paul Johnston is curator of Maritime History at the Smithsonian's Museum of American History here in Washington, D.C. The museum displays the gold nugget Mr Marshall found.

Paul Johnston: And you can see Mr Marshall actually bit down on it. You can see the molar marks, his bite mark on it as well as a little chip taken out of the upper left hand corner for assaying, or testing the purity of the gold.

Speaker: Mr Marshall knew he found gold because the metal was soft. He and his boss gave the nugget to the US government to prove they found gold on the land. News of James Marshall's discovery traveled to the East Coast. But communication was slow in the middle of the 19th century. People in the big eastern cities of New York and Boston heard only rumors about gold in California. It was not until December 1848, almost a year after Mr Marshall's discovery, that President James Polk told Congress the rumors were true. During the next weeks and months, thousands of young men from the Northeast left their homes and families to seek great riches in California.

Paul Johnston: You didn't really have to work for it, as far as they knew. You just had to lean over and pick it up and you were rich.

Speaker: One of those young men was Benjamin Buckley. His records suggest he found thousands of dollars' worth of gold. Buckley put some money in banks and sent some to family members. Alexander Van Valen, however, was not as successful. The Smithsonian's Museum of American History has letters he wrote to his wife and daughters in New York.

Paul Johnston: His wife tried to make a living by sewing and by borrowing money from the financiers against her husband's future profits. But it was not any easier for her than it was for her husband 3,000 miles away in California.

Speaker: In two years, Alexander Van Valen earned only $ 500. Most people who traveled to California to find gold were like Van Valen – they did not get rich. But Paul Johnston says the California Gold Rush was important for other reasons.

Paul Johnston: The Gold Rush really put California on the map. It made it desirable. It made the East Coast want California to become part of the United States. So, it was huge.

Speaker: In 1850, California became the country's 31st state.

Adapted from: https://learningenglish.voanews.com/a/california-gold-rush-1849/1969067.html

Listening Test 5: Route 66

Speaker: On November 11, 1926, a 3,900 km long highway was established in the United States. It was not the first American highway. It was not the longest either. And it might not have been the fastest. But the road inspired musicians, writers and filmmakers. It appealed to explorers and dreamers. It's known as the Route 66. The road cuts through cornfields, deserts, mountains and unusual red rock formations of the west. As the scene outside the car window changes, so, too, do the people and cultures found along the road.
It was disaster that fuelled the road's early success. A series of powerful dust storms in the 1930s destroyed a huge amount of farmland across the prairie states. Hundreds of thousands of mostly poor farm workers and their families began to leave. The migrants headed west on Route 66, hoping the path would lead to a better life in California, the land of opportunity. Exploring the open road has long been an important part of the American experience. And Route 66 became even more popular as the car culture exploded in the 1940s and 50s. However, by the 1960s, large parts of Route 66 were not fit for driving.
The U.S. government built bigger highways, with faster speed limits and fewer traffic lights. These new interstates bypassed small towns, the heart of Route 66. Many of these small towns had depended on Route 66 for business and income. The economies of bypassed small towns suffered. When the traffic stopped on Route 66, so did many of the towns themselves.

Abridged and adapted from: Ashley Thompson and Caty Weaver: Route 66: 'The Highway that's The Best', in: Voice of America Learning English

Listening Test 6: Things you didn't know about London

Speaker: Everyone knows London, don't they? But I wonder how many of you know some of the facts I'm going to tell you.
There are over eight million people who live in London and these people speak 300 different languages. And every year, London gets an average of 17 million visitors – perhaps you were one of them? If you were, then maybe you know that every year Oslo, the capital of Norway, gives London a big Christmas tree for Trafalgar Square.
You've heard of Big Ben and you'll know it's not really the name of the tower but only of the bell inside it. However, only few people know that the Houses of Parliament still have a strange law: you're not allowed to enter the building wearing a suit of armour. I can just imagine people doing that today, can't you?
Have you heard of Peter Pan? Of course there have been lots of books and films about him. But did you know that all the royalties from the books and the films go to a children's hospital in London called Great Ormond Street? Royalties are a percentage of the book price or the ticket price to see

a film or a play. The author, James Matthew Barrie, didn't have any children himself, so when he died, he gave the hospital this present, which has made it quite rich.

London had the very first underground railway in the world, but there were some unexpected surprises for the workers when building it. At Aldgate Station, for example, they discovered a huge grave with 1,000 dead bodies in it from the plague of 1665. They decided to continue building the station above the bodies rather than removing them all! They're still there!

London is slowly growing upwards rather than outwards and you only have to look at its skyline to see this. One of the most interesting buildings is the Shard. You can't miss it, because it's 310 metres high. Many of London's high-rise buildings have been given fun names such as the Gherkin, the Cheese Grater or the Walkie-Talkie. Look out for them next time you're in London.

Listening Test 7: Say no to plastic!

Richard: Hi, Lucy. It's good you're here today on White Rose Radio.

Lucy: Thanks for having me.

Richard: You wanted to tell our listeners about your fight against plastic and how it all began. Am I right?

Lucy: Yes, you are. It's something that slowly developed. My family were at the coast last year and the beach was covered in plastic bottles and lots of other rubbish. Later, I read about how polluted the sea is by plastic … and then I read that a plastic spoon only takes a few seconds to make, and after it's used it's just thrown away. But what most people don't know is that it'll then need 500 to 1,000 years before it has decomposed.

Richard: I didn't know that … and I guess it's the same story for plastic knives and forks, isn't it?

Lucy: Sure is. But I also watched a video about making a plastic spoon. The chemicals were taken from Europe to China, the spoon was made there, then wrapped up in plastic with millions of others and taken by boat to America. The spoons were then put onto large lorries, which took them to a distribution centre, and then smaller vans took them to cafés and hotels. So, one spoon travelled around the world! How environmentally friendly is that? Can't we just wash metal ones?

Richard: I often think that, too. And I get angry about plastic bags.

Lucy: I do, too. In England, a plastic bag costs 5 pence if you want one – 50 pence would be better. But, why don't shops just change to paper bags?

Richard: I agree. I always take my own bag to the supermarket. But if I buy clothes I don't want to put them in this bag. I hate it when the shop then gives me a plastic bag instead of a paper one.

Lucy: Take-away-coffee cups are another problem.

Richard: Are they? I thought you could recycle them.

Lucy: Not really. They're made of paper but the cups have a special type of plastic inside them. This plastic is very difficult to separate from the paper.

In the UK there are only three factories that can do this, so only about 1 % of all the coffee cups are recycled.

Richard: That's terrible.

Lucy: It is. I read that 500,000 coffee cups in the UK are thrown away every day and 99 % of them aren't recycled.

Richard: Is anyone dealing with this problem?

Lucy: A lot of the coffee outlets are starting to take some action at last. But there are many interesting ideas about how to deal with the problem, too. For example, to replace the paper cups with containers made of glass, metal, ceramic or bamboo.

Richard: How would that work? Wouldn't that cost a lot of money because people would just throw those away, too?

Lucy: Not really because you would have to pay extra for the coffee container, then you can take it away with you. When it is empty, you can return it to any coffee shop where you get your money back and the container can be washed and used again – just like a cup in a restaurant.

Richard: I like that idea. Thanks for coming on the programme today, Lucy. Let's hope we all see less plastic used everywhere – and very soon, too.

Listening Test 8: Booking a hotel room

Receptionist: The Old Waverley Hotel in Edinburgh. This is Lewis Breckenridge speaking. How may I help you?

Sophie: Hello. This is Sophie Burns. I'd like to book a hotel room for my parents for their silver wedding anniversary. It's a surprise.

Receptionist: Oh, wow, your parents have been married for 25 years! What a great idea to send them to Edinburgh on a romantic trip. Can you give me the dates, please?

Sophie: Yes, I hope they like it! Ah, it's from 15th to 18th August.

Receptionist: OK. I'll just check if we've got any vacancies at that time – August is usually really busy, you know, because of the Fringe Festival. Just a moment, please … Ah, you're extremely lucky. We've just had a cancellation. There's only one room left.

Sophie: That's fantastic. What type of room is it and how much does it cost?

Receptionist: It's a beautiful large double room with a fantastic view of Edinburgh Castle. Unfortunately, prices are up in August, so it's £ 165 per night for the room.

Sophie: Oh … I'm afraid I can't afford that.

Receptionist: Ah … well, just to let you know: we've usually got special offers for the winter months. So if it were possible for your parents to travel, say, in December, you could, for example, book dinner and a full English breakfast for them in our restaurant at full price and you'd only have to pay £ 1 per person per night!

Sophie: That sounds great. I'll think about it. Thank you so much for the information.

Receptionist: You're very welcome. If you're interested, I could put you on our mailing list for our monthly newsletter. So you wouldn't miss any of our special offers.

Sophie: Hmm, why not. Here's my e-mail address: sburns.15@openmail.co.uk. That is s-b-u-r-n-s.15@o-p-e-n-m-a-i-l.c-o.u-k.

Receptionist: Thank you, I've got that. You should get an e-mail from us in the next few minutes. Just click on the link to confirm that you would like to receive our newsletters.

Sophie: OK, thank you so much for your help. Bye-bye.

Receptionist: Bye-bye, Ms Burns.

Listening Test 9: The Stolen Generations

Greg: This is *TopFM*, my name is Greg and I'd like to welcome you to our special programme on the history of Australia. Jenny Green has come into the studio today to talk about the so-called Stolen Generations. Jenny, could you explain to our listeners what happened to these people?

Jenny: Sure. From the late nineteenth century to about 1970, various Australian governments took Aboriginal children – or children who had at least one Aboriginal parent – away from their families. Their aim was to make them adopt white culture.

Greg: What was the idea behind that?

Jenny: Well, basically, the governments were trying to get rid of Aboriginal peoples and their traditions. They thought that if Aboriginal children were forced to adopt white culture, the Aboriginal way of life would soon die out.

Greg: But Aboriginal peoples had been there long before the first Europeans arrived.

Jenny: That's true, of course, but many whites thought their culture was better than that of the Aboriginal peoples.

Greg: What happened to the children?

Jenny: The children were separated from their parents – their families – and often taken thousands of miles away, so they would never see each other again. You can imagine how awful this was for them. Many children were also told that their parents had died or just left them. These children were then put into homes run by the church or the state. Some were also adopted from the homes by white families. Most were given "white" names and the only language they were allowed to use was English, not their own – that was forbidden. They were taught to reject their Aboriginal past.

Greg: Sounds like something out of a bad film ...

Jenny: But, sadly, it was for real. In some areas, one in three children were taken away – nearly every Aboriginal family lost children in this way. In the homes, children were badly treated and often left cold and hungry. They were given an education, but usually a rather poor one – one just enough to allow them to do basic work, for example as household servants or shepherds.

Greg: Things must have got better since then, though.

Jenny: Yes, but it's taken a long time. In 1997, there was a critical report of what happened to the Stolen Generations. One of its suggestions was to have an annual National Sorry Day for all Australians to remember this part of their country's history – it was later renamed the National Day of Healing. In 2000, during the Olympic Games in Sydney, an Aboriginal runner was chosen to light the Olympic fire. After winning a gold medal, she ran around the track carrying both the Aboriginal flag and the Australian one – a powerful symbol of reconciliation. But it wasn't until 2008 that an Australian prime minister officially apologised to the Stolen Generations.

Greg: So has the sad history of the Stolen Generations finally come to an end?

Jenny: Unfortunately, not completely. Many Aboriginal people still suffer from how they were treated by the whites. And apparently, the number of children who are taken away from their parents is still much higher for Aboriginal people than for white people. Even today, governments seem to spend a lot more money on putting Aboriginal children into state-run homes than on helping them to stay with their parents.

Greg: These aren't very happy facts, are they? Well thanks for now, Jenny, and we'll talk some more after the break …

Listening Test 10: Part-time jobs

Reporter: Good morning, ladies and gentlemen. This is Poppy Mitchell and I'm reporting live from Forrester High School. Today I'm trying to find out what kinds of jobs pupils do to earn some extra money. My first interview partner here is seventeen-year-old Lexi. Lexi, do you have a part-time job?

Lexi: Yes, I do. I'm a babysitter. I usually work every Friday and Saturday afternoon, and sometimes in the evenings, too. It's the best job I can imagine, because it never gets boring. I love kids and playing with them. I look after our neighbours' children. They're two, five and eight years old.

Marc: My name's Marc and I'm sixteen. I don't have a part-time job right now. I used to work for a pizza delivery service for a few months and I really liked it. It was my job to buy the ingredients at the markets, but I also had to work in the kitchen or even deliver the pizzas. My parents made me quit two weeks ago, because my marks are too bad in Maths.

Leo: I'm Leo, I'm sixteen, too, and I'm a Maths tutor. If you want, I can help you improve your marks, Marc. My rates are affordable for everyone.
I do private and group tutorials and the feedback I get is really good, because I'm patient and I always prepare my own material. I want to become a Maths teacher in the future.

Reporter: Thank you all for answering my questions honestly. I wish you all the best for your future.

Original-Prüfungsaufgaben

Abschlussarbeiten an der IGS in Niedersachsen
Englisch 2021

E-Kurs

I. Listening

Part 1 – Questions 1–7

7 Punkte

Listen to seven short recordings. For each recording, there is a question with three pictures. Choose the correct picture and put a tick (✓) in the box A, B or C below it.

Example

0. What is the man going to buy?

A ☐ B ☐ C ☑

1. Which road should you take into London?

A ☐ B ☐ C ☐

2. What does the guest order?

A ☐ B ☐ C ☐

3. Which app is Casey looking for?

A ☐ B ☐ C ☐

4. What type of transportation does the couple choose?

A ☐

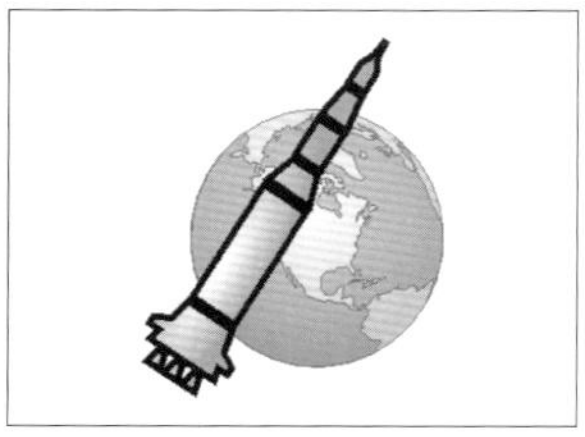

B ☐

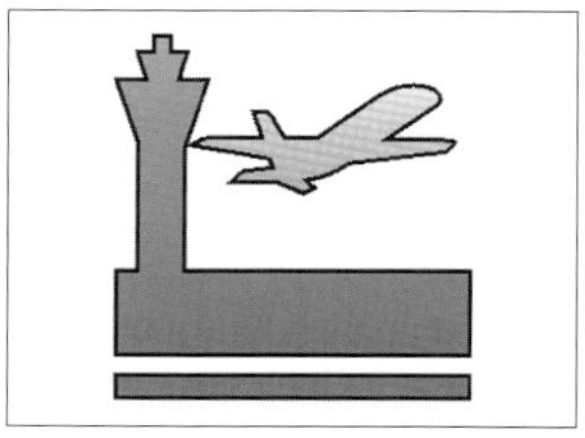

C ☐

5. How does the customer pay?

A ☐

B ☐

C ☐

6. Which stamp does the woman buy?

A ☐

B ☐

C ☐

7. What is their plan for the weekend?

A ☐

B ☐

C ☐

Part 2 – Questions 8–13: Apartment Viewing

Listen to Peter Schmidt talking to a real-estate agent while looking at an apartment. For each question, tick (✓) the correct box a, b or c.

6 Punkte

8. The kitchen is …
   a) a separate room. ☐
   b) old-fashioned. ☐
   c) fully equipped. ☐

9. Peter Schmidt would …
   a) need to bring his own furniture. ☐
   b) be able to move in with his own couch. ☐
   c) be allowed to use the apartment's TV. ☐

10. The apartment has …
    a) two bedrooms that share a closet. ☐
    b) more than one kitchen. ☐
    c) a room with a washing machine. ☐

11. The rent …
    a) is paid every three months. ☐
    b) covers no additional costs. ☐
    c) includes the cost of the Internet. ☐

12. Peter Schmidt might move in …
    a) if the landlord chooses him. ☐
    b) in two weeks. ☐
    c) after completing his renovation work. ☐

13. The application form must …
    a) include a reference. ☐
    b) be sent to Peter Schmidt's employer. ☐
    c) reach the office before the weekend. ☐

Part 3 – Questions 14–20: Power Skates

7 Punkte

You are interested in a pair of Power Skates.
You listen to a commercial to find out more about them.
Fill in the missing information.
The first question is an example.

Name of the product:	0. Power Skates
Powered by:	14. ______
Max. range:	15. ______
How to learn:	16. ______
Max. speed:	17. ______
How to control speed:	18. ______
Discount price:	19. ______
Coupon code:	20. ______

Part 4 – Questions 21–26: Returning from Germany

6 Punkte

You will hear a radio interview with Noah Clarkson, an American teenager who has just returned from spending a year in Germany as an exchange student.
Decide whether each statement is true or false and put a tick (✓) in the correct box.
The first question is an example.

	Statement	true	false
0.	Emily Sanders spent a year in Germany.	☐	✓
21.	Noah's great-grandfather lives in Germany.	☐	☐
22.	Noah disliked public transportation in Germany.	☐	☐
23.	Noah travelled to cities outside of Germany.	☐	☐
24.	Noah thinks American food is less healthy than European food.	☐	☐
25.	Noah thinks most Germans are reserved when you first meet them.	☐	☐
26.	Noah is going to visit some German friends this summer.	☐	☐

II. Reading

Part 1 – Questions 1–6: Short texts

6 Punkte

Read the texts below and read the statements 1–6.
Decide whether the statements are true or false. Then tick (✓) the correct box.

1.

Teacher for extracurricular activities at Triangle Lake Elementary School

We are looking for teachers, counselors, and coaches, who offer musical, creative, academic or athletic programs and clubs for our students.

Pay: up to $30 per hour depending on qualifications
Working hours: 3–5 p.m. Mon–Thu during school weeks

Experience and qualifications favored, but not needed.

Applications to school office:
TLS, School Road, Blachly

2.

Youth Service Office London

Due to water damage our office is closed indefinitely!!!

In urgent cases we will arrange appointments in the family centre in Zach Street.

Please contact us by email or phone! (contact below).

Our letter box is still cleared daily.

Phone: 020-39 34 89
Email: ysol@london.co.uk

3.

Do you need help running your errands?

I am George, a sixteen-year-old student, trying to save money for a year abroad. Very reliable and motivated.

I offer:
Grocery shopping
Walking your dog
Office courses
Help in the garden
And much more

Available times:
Weekdays from 5–7 pm,
Saturdays from 10 am – 4 pm

From £7 depending on job.

4.

Band members wanted for Indie Rock project: "Aim 42"

Looking for bassist and drummer!

Bassist: Strong riffy bass that can fill some space. Ability to chord progression is a must.

Drummer: Must know when slow and simple is appropriate while still being able to play accurately at higher speeds.

Rehearsals: Every Wednesday at 9 pm at basement of Cedar Creek public swimming pools.

Understanding of music theory required.

Contact us on Insta if interested: @Aim_42

		true	false
1.	On Tuesdays George can walk your dog in the morning and in the afternoon.	☐	☐
2.	The elementary school is looking for experienced teachers only.	☐	☐
3.	As a new band member, you have to be able to read music.	☐	☐
4.	The Youth Service Office can still be reached by post.	☐	☐
5.	The band meets once a week to practice.	☐	☐
6.	The teaching wage is the same for everybody.	☐	☐

Part 2 – Questions 7–13: Charlene Rocha – A Teen Activist

7 Punkte

Read the answers teen activist Charlene Rocha has given in an interview. Below the answers there are eight questions. Decide which question is most suitable for each answer. For texts 7–13 write the correct letter A–H in the box next to the number. There are more questions than answers. Each letter can only be used once.

7. ☐ There are so many more components to it than people think! I'm currently working with a committee called Break the Chains and we are fighting against anti-Black racism. We held a protest in Pickering, Ontario that was about two hours long, but behind-the-scenes there were many more hours of emailing, discussions, writing, and researching!

8. ☐ The first time I learned about it was through a speaker that came to my school. She told us about the effects climate change was causing in poorer countries. I was completely in shock that we could have such a huge problem in the world and have governments still refusing to act. I felt motivated to do something.

9. ☐ I enjoy celebrating the world we are saving! I go on hikes with my friends, rollerblade with my sister, take my dog for long walks, and swim at the beach. Activism isn't supposed to be super stressful – it's a fun thing to do!

10. ☐ Find a cause that you are passionate about and research it! Knowing the facts is an important factor to effective activism. Whether it's reading a book, or listening to the news, knowing about these issues is a great way to get involved and inspire other people around you too.

11. ☐ It was a rush of emotions. I did a speech completely on the spot and it definitely was spontaneous. I was a pretty quiet person before I became an activist, so this was definitely something that shocked my friends, family, and me!

12. ☐ Sometimes I get nervous, forget what to say, and make mistakes. But that is completely okay! The way that I've learned to handle speeches is by reminding myself that it's just a speech. Even if I do seem nervous, I will learn and grow from it.

13. ☐ Everything is connected. For example, Black and Indigenous people are affected the most by climate change in Canada. This means that in addressing one issue, you are fighting for another one as well.

A What did it feel like speaking at a *FridaysForFuture* event when you were 13?

B How do you handle speaking in front of a large crowd?

C When did you first become aware of environmental activism?

D Besides protests and giving speeches, what else is there to activism?

E What do you do to relax and wind down?

F Why do you fight for so many things at once?

G What is your next big project?

H What is a great first step for kids to make activism a part of their lives?

Adapted from: Teen activist Charlene Rocha/OWLconnected, 02. 07. 2020,
http://owlconnected.com/archives/interview-charlene-rocha

Part 3 – Questions 14–19: Why Teenagers Really Do Need an Extra Hour in Bed

6 Punkte

Read the following article about the sleep needs of adolescents.
For questions 14–19, tick (✓) the correct box a, b or c.
For each question there is only one correct answer.

The biology of human sleep timing changes as we age. As puberty begins, bedtimes and waking times get later. This trend continues until 19.5 years in women and 21 in men. Then it reverses. At 55 we wake at about the time we woke prior to puberty. On average this is two hours earlier than adolescents. This means that for a teenager, a 7 am alarm call is the equivalent of a 5 am start for a person in their 50s.

However, biology is only part of the problem. Additional factors include a more relaxed attitude to bedtimes by parents, a general disregard for the importance of sleep, and access to electronic devices, which keep teenagers awake. The amount of sleep teenagers get varies between countries, geographic region and social class, but all studies show they are going to bed later and not getting as much sleep as they need because of early school starts.

Sleep scientists have shown that teenagers need about nine hours a night to maintain full alertness and academic performance. But in reality, many were getting just five hours of sleep on school days. Unsurprisingly, teachers reported students being tired in class.

In the US, the observation that teenagers have biologically delayed sleep patterns compared to adults prompted several schools to put back the start of the school day. An analysis found that academic performance was enhanced, as was attendance. In the UK, Monkseaton High School near Newcastle instituted a 10 am start in 2009 and saw an uptick in academic performance.

However, a later start by itself is not enough. Society in general, and teenagers in particular, must start to take sleep seriously.

If you are dependent upon an alarm clock, or parent, to get you out of bed; if you take a long time to wake up; if you feel sleepy and irritable during the day; if your behaviour is overly impulsive, it means you are probably not getting enough sleep. Take control. Ensure the bedroom is a place that promotes sleep – dark and not warm – don't look at electric screens for at least half an hour before trying to sleep and avoid bright lights. Seek out natural light in the morning to adjust the body clock and sleep patterns to an earlier time.

Adapted from: Russell Foster: Why teenagers really do need an extra hour in bed, New Scientist, 17.04.2013, https://www.newscientist.com/article/mg21829130-100-why-teenagers-really-do-need-an-extra-hour-in-bed/#ixzz6aGjzT0Wf

14. Sleeping time …
    a) is consistent through life. ☐
    b) starts later with puberty. ☐
    c) ends later for seniors. ☐

15. For teenagers an alarm at 7 am feels …
    a) later than for 50-year-olds. ☐
    b) the same as for 50-year-olds. ☐
    c) like a 5 am alarm for 50-year-olds. ☐

16. According to the article, teenagers often get too little sleep because …
    a) their parents go to bed too late as well. ☐
    b) they think sleep is unimportant. ☐
    c) they are often woken by their smartphones. ☐

17. To realize their full potential at school, teenagers should …
    a) sleep around nine hours per night. ☐
    b) set an early alarm. ☐
    c) rest for five hours after school. ☐

18. After starting times were delayed at some schools …
    a) students' performance got worse. ☐
    b) more students were present in class. ☐
    c) students began to take sleep more seriously. ☐

19. For better sleep …
    a) your bedroom should be warm and dark. ☐
    b) avoid looking at your smartphone before bedtime. ☐
    c) seek out natural light right before going to bed. ☐

Part 4 – Questions 20–26: Dutee Chand – An Indian Sprint Star's Rapid Rise

7 Punkte

Read the article about the Indian athlete Dutee Chand. For questions 20–26, tick (✓) the correct box true *or* false *<u>and</u> give the line(s) of reference in the text. The first question is an example.*

Sprinter Dutee Chand is India's national champion at 100 m and at Rio 2016 became only the third Indian woman to qualify for the women's Olympic 100 m. The 23-year-old talks about her financial hardship as an aspiring athlete and the controversy she has had to overcome in her eventful career: "People around the world see me running for just 10–12 seconds. But no one knows that to run these seconds, I have to train 365 days a year." Dutee Chand is one of South Asia's fastest running female sprinters competing in the 100 m. "If you don't win, people will forget you. So, you always have to win. And you have to work very hard for it. I train six times a day. During our workout we have to do repetitions of 100–500 m sprints." Last year, Dutee clocked her career-best time at 11.22 seconds.

She was inspired by her sister who was a state-level runner. "I never dreamt of becoming an internationally successful runner. But then my sister told me that if I took up running, I would be able to support my education. So, to keep my studies going I started running. But I faced a lot of problems. I had no running shoes and no money to buy any. There were no proper running tracks to practise on. No good coaches. So I started running alone in my village, barefoot, on the river bank and on the road. My diet consisted of whatever was cooked at home."

Dutee Chand had to overcome many financial hardships to succeed. Sometimes she even spent the nights on railway platforms because she had no money to pay for a hotel. Then, in 2014, she was accused of doping because the level of male hormones in her blood was higher than normal. Therefore, she was excluded from participating in the Commonwealth Games. But she appealed to an international court. "Everyone has hormones", she says, "some have more and some have less. Was it my fault?" Eventually, she won the case and was allowed to participate.

The ban affected her preparations for the 2016 Olympic Games. At the 2017 Asian Championship, Chand won two bronze medals. But her biggest success so far came in 2018 during the Asian Games when Dutee won two silver medals in the 100 and 200 meters. She is currently aiming at a podium finish in the 2021 Tokyo Olympics.

Adapted from: BBC Indian Sportswoman of the Year: Dutee Chand, Reporter: Rakhee Sharma, 03. 02. 2020, https://www.bbc.com/sport/av/51107178

		true	false	line(s)
0.	Dutee Chand is a national sprint champion from India.	☑	☐	1
20.	She was the first Indian woman to qualify for the Olympics.	☐	☐	___
21.	Dutee trains several times a day.	☐	☐	___
22.	She completed her fastest 100 m run in under eleven seconds.	☐	☐	___
23.	Her sister was internationally successful as a runner.	☐	☐	___
24.	Dutee used to train barefoot because she was too poor to buy running shoes.	☐	☐	___
25.	She was banned from the Commonwealth Games for possible doping in 2014.	☐	☐	___
26.	In 2018, Dutee won two silver medals at the Asian Games.	☐	☐	___

III. Writing – Set I

Part 1 – Feedback: London City Tour

10 Punkte

You have just finished a guided city tour of London. You rated the tour and the guide in five categories as seen in the table.

Leave feedback in which you explain your ratings.

Write about 80 words.

Friendliness	★★★★
Entertainment	★★★☆
Interesting information	★★★★
Selection of sights	★★☆☆
Overall impression	★★★☆

Part 2 – An E-Mail: International School Competition

Inhalt: 9 Punkte
Sprache: 9 Punkte
Gesamt: 18 Punkte

You have found the following competition on the website of Schools United. Write an entry for the competition in about 150 words.

Tell us what $ 50,000 could do for your school.
You can win the money for your school if you convince us!

Include these aspects:
- *a short introduction to your school*
- *what needs to be better*
- *how you would spend the money*

TO: competition@schoolsunited.com

SUBJECT: $ 50,000 for my school

Dear Schools United,

III. Writing – Set II

Part 1 – A Report: Stolen Bike

10 Punkte

Your bike was stolen, and you reported the theft to the police. The police asked you to write a short report including the following:

- *Where and when you left your bike*
- *A detailed description of your bike*
- *Whether your bike was registered and locked*

Write about 80 words.

Part 2 – A Blog Entry: My Trip to Mars

Inhalt: 9 Punkte
Sprache: 9 Punkte
Gesamt: 18 Punkte

Imagine you live in the year 2050. You have just returned from a trip to planet Mars. Write a blog entry about the trip.

In your text include:

- *How you travelled and what the journey was like*
- *What life is like on Mars*
- *What you missed there and what you are now missing on Earth*

Write about 150 words.

Anhang – Hörverstehenstexte: E-Kurs

This is the listening part of the final examination 2021 level B 1 for schools in Lower Saxony. There are four parts to the test. You will hear each recording twice. For each part of the test there will be time for you to look through the questions. You must not speak during the test.

Part 1

Now look at part 1, questions 1 to 7. Listen to seven short recordings. For each recording, there is a question with three pictures. Choose the correct picture and put a tick in the box A, B or C below it. Before we start, here is an example.

Example

What is the man going to buy?

Man: I'm going shopping now. Anything else we need for our holiday?

Woman: The sunscreen from our last trip should still work. I haven't got any sunglasses, but I can borrow some of yours, can't I? Hm, maybe something to kill the time at the airport.

Man: Yes. That's a good idea. I'll stop by the newsagent's.

The picture with the magazine is correct. So there is a tick in box C.

Text 1

Look at the three pictures for question 1 now.
Now we are ready to start. Listen carefully.

Which road should you take into London?

Traffic is crazy this morning. Here's an update for all drivers trying to get into the city. There's serious congestion on the M1 southbound at junction four at Elstree. You have to expect delays of at least an hour if you're on the M1.
Our advice is to get off at junction five and take the A41. The A1 is also quite busy. It's not an alternative today. Have a safe journey.

Now listen again.

Text 2

What does the guest order?

Waiter: So, have you made up your mind? Let me tell you, the ribeye steak is awesome.

Woman: Well, I was just looking at the Caesar salad. Does it come with chicken?

Waiter: We can do that. Is that what you want? That'd be three dollars extra.

Woman: You know what? I think I'm going for your recommendation.

Waiter: Good call, ma'am.

Now listen again.

Text 3

Which app is Casey looking for?

Casey: Hey, Jeff, what was that app called that you told me about the other day?
Jeff: Hey, Casey, do you mean "Find My Lover"? That's a nifty dating app.
Casey: Hmm. I think it had to do with sharing your calendar with others.
Jeff: Share your calendar? You can share events with the default calendar app.
Casey: Yeah, I know that.
Jeff: Well, with "Cal-Export", you can print your calendar so that you put it on your wall old-fashioned style.
Casey: Or give it to others. That's what I was thinking of. Thanks.

Now listen again.

Text 4

What type of transportation does the couple choose?

Man: Honey, we've never been on a cruise. It's always been my dream to cross the pond on one.
Woman: That's because I get seasick, honey. Huh. But how would you feel about city hopping across Europe?
Man: Only if we get there on a cruise or by rocket. That's a thing now, isn't it?
Woman: Oh, come on. Very funny. Like I wouldn't get sick on a rocket.
Man: All right, then. But I'll tell the pilot to try and fly as fast as one.
Woman: It's gonna be awesome.

Now listen again.

Text 5

How does the customer pay?

Sales clerk: All right, that's 4.99, please.
Customer: Ah, there you go.
Sales clerk: Oh, I'm sorry, we're cash free.
Customer: Oh, OK. Shoot, I don't have a card with me. Oh, well, then this should work.
Sales clerk: Thank you very much. Have a great day.

Text 6

Which stamp does the woman buy?

Woman: I need a stamp, please.
Man: Sure. Which one do you need? 60, 75 or 90?
Woman: It's for a postcard to Germany. So 90, I guess.
Man: 60 is for national, 75 for international postcards and 90 is for letters. Here's the one you need.

Text 7

What is their plan for the weekend?

Mother: Hey, it's our family weekend coming up. What would you like to do?

Boy: Mom, let's go to the Mighty Midland's Park. There's a new crazy roller coaster.

Mother: Hm. Crazy idea, but it's also crazy expensive.

Boy: Why don't we go for a walk in the forest then?

Mother: Really? I'd love that.

Boy: I was just kidding. It's the last chance to see *In the Dark Light* on the big screen. So we don't actually have a choice, Mom.

Now listen again.

This is the end of part 1.

Part 2

Now turn to part 2, questions 8 to 13. Listen to Peter Schmidt talking to a real estate agent while looking at an apartment. For each question tick the correct box, a, b or c.
Now you have 30 seconds to look at part 2.
Now we are ready to start. Listen carefully.

Woman: Hi, Peter Schmidt from Germany, how are you doing?

Peter: I'm fine, thanks. Yes, that's correct. I'm interested in the apartment.

Woman: Awesome. Well, let's go right in. And here we are. This is the spacious living area with a modern open kitchen to our left. It has all the latest appliances. The fridge has a built-in screen to show you recipes and what groceries you need.

Peter: Uh huh. That's nice. Oh, and there's a sofa. Does it belong to the apartment?

Woman: Yes, the apartment is furnished. Everything you see here is included. If you want to bring your own couch, you'd have to store this one away. You bring your own TV set, computer and stuff. But there are loads of power outlets for all your devices.

Peter: I see it all looks very nice and is in good condition. So how many rooms are there overall?

Woman: Well, it's a two-bedroom apartment. Both bedrooms have their own closet. Then there's one bathroom with a shower bath and the kitchen has a pantry attached. And over there is a laundry room for your clothes. It has a dryer, too.

Peter: What about the rent?

Woman: The rent for the apartment is 210 dollars per week. You pay at the beginning of the month. Then there are the additional costs for maintenance, electricity and so on. This is paid quarterly and it's currently around three hundred dollars. Internet and cable are not included.

Peter: OK, and when is the apartment available?

Woman: Very soon. The landlord wants to choose his new tenant in about two weeks, depending on the renovation work that will be done in the first week of June. I would say that end of June should be possible.

Peter: OK, great. I'm interested. How do I apply?

Woman: All you have to do is fill in this application form. Of course it can help to show a reference from your current employer or someone like that, but please make sure to get your form to our office by Friday.

Peter: All right, I can do that. Thank you very much.

Woman: I'm keeping my fingers crossed for you. Good-bye, Peter.

Now listen again.

This is the end of part 2.

Part 3

Now turn to part 3, questions 14 to 20 – Power Skates. You are interested in a pair of Power Skates. You listen to a commercial to find out more about them. Fill in the missing information. The first question is an example. You have 20 seconds to look at part 3.
Now we are ready to start. Listen carefully.

(Jingle: Power Skates) Have you ever dreamed of gliding along the street without any physical effort? Then this dream is about to come true with Power Skates *(Jingle)*. You don't only get to your destination quickly, it's fun too. Power Skates are skates powered by a rechargeable battery. Charge them anywhere. Just hook them up to your household outlet. In only 20 minutes, your Power Skates are charged enough for you to glide two miles and your Power Skates are fully charged in sixty minutes. You can go up to six miles on a single charge. *(Jingle)*

Is it difficult to ride them? Not at all. It's super easy and super safe. Our free app offers a great video tutorial for you to learn how to ride your Power Skates safely. For the first 20 miles your speed is limited to five miles an hour to start slowly and safely. As soon as you're more experienced, you are able to go full speed at 15 miles an hour. What do you get when you purchase Power Skates today? Your super sleek Power Skates come with a powerful charger and with a super precise remote control. That's what you use to control your Power Skates: speed and light. That's right. You can make your Power Skates light up in a variety of great colors. If you think Power Skates are expensive, you're wrong. You can get your Powers Skates for only 399 dollars at your local store. But wait, if you buy your pair on our website www.powerskates.com today, you'll get a 50 dollar discount. All you have to do is enter our voucher code when you check out. That's right. You'll get your Power Skates for only 349 dollars.

The voucher code is "safeandfun21". I'll say it again: "safeandfun21". Your Power Skates are waiting for you. Order them now. *(Jingle)*

Due to occasional shortages, some sizes may not be in stock.

Now listen again. [...] This is the end of part 3.

Part 4

Now turn to part 4, questions 21 to 26. You will hear a radio interview with Noah Clarkson, an American teenager who has just returned from spending a year in Germany as an exchange student. Decide whether each statement is true or false and put a tick in the correct box. The first question is an example. You now have 30 seconds to look at part 4.
Now we are ready to start. Listen carefully. You will hear the recording twice.

Radio host: Good morning, listeners. My name is Emily Sanders, and with me today is Noah Clarkson. He's 18 years old and he just returned from a year in Germany as an exchange student. Noah, why did you choose to go to Germany? And was it a good decision?

Noah: Hey, thanks for having me on the show. Oh, it was the best decision of my life. Well, so far *(laughs)*. I absolutely loved it in Germany. And I'll definitely go back. I decided to go to Germany because my great-grandfather immigrated from there. So, I've always been curious what life's like there.

Radio host: And what is it like? And what is it that you like about Germany?

Noah: There are many things that Germany seems to do right and that make living awesome there. First, I love public transportation there. Here in the States, everyone uses their cars and you hardly ever see buses or trains. Kind of sad! In Germany, public transportation is such a big thing. You're able to skip the traffic and five or six minutes later, you're at the stop where you want to be. And on the bus or the train, you can just relax. It's insane. It's super clean, super chill.

Radio host: And obviously it's good for the environment. Did you travel around a lot?

Noah: Yeah, that's another cool thing. Germany is right in the middle of where you want to be in Europe. You hop on a plane or train and within a few hours you're in another great place in Europe. I went to Lisbon in two and a half hours or so. You're in another great country. You can use the same money and everything's so easy.

Radio host: I see. What about the food? How did you like that in Germany?

Noah: The food is superb. Every one in Europe. They're all mixed into Germany. You have Mediterranean food, Italian food, Turkish food, and it all tastes so original, the best that it can. Here in America, the food is so oily and has chemicals in it, I think. In Germany, I eat and I feel fit afterwards.

Radio host: I'm sure you made some friends over there. Do you keep in touch?

Noah: Yes, well, here's the thing about people in America and in Germany. I feel like people in America are more outgoing but at the same time more selfish maybe. Of course, this is stereotypes, but Germans seem kind of cold at first. But once you get past that first wall of cold, and you actually become friends with them, that's when you notice how loyal and respectful they are to you. It's likely that when you are friends with a German, you're going to be friends with them for a very, very long time. Of course, not all Germans are like that and not all Americans are superficial, but it's still an impression that I have. So, yeah, my host brother and a friend are coming to visit me over summer. I'm really looking forward to that.

Radio host: Noah, thank you for sharing your impressions with us. It's always interesting to hear about other countries. Now, coming up, some music from some of the … *(fade out)*

Now listen again.

This is the end of the listening part. Good luck for the rest of your examination!

G-Kurs

I. Listening

Part 1 – Questions 1–7

7 Punkte

You will hear seven short conversations. You will hear each conversation twice.
For each question there are three pictures and a short recording.
Choose the correct picture and put a tick (✓) in the box below it.

Example

0. Which tickets do they buy?

A ☐

B ☐

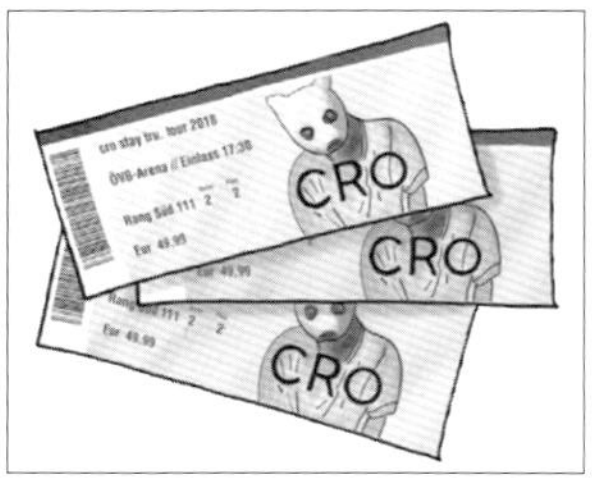

C ☑

1. When does the training take place?

A ☐

B ☐

C ☐

2. Which film do they want to watch?

A ☐

B ☐

C ☐

3. Which main course do they order?

A ☐

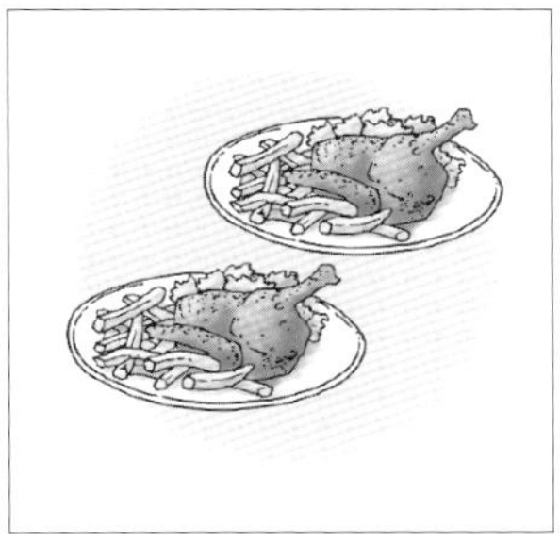
B ☐

C ☐

4. What problem does the man have?

A ☐

B ☐

C ☐

5. Which road should you take into London?

A ☐

B ☐

C ☐

6. At what time do the women meet?

A ☐

B ☐

C ☐

7. What kind of music will they have at their graduation party?

A ☐

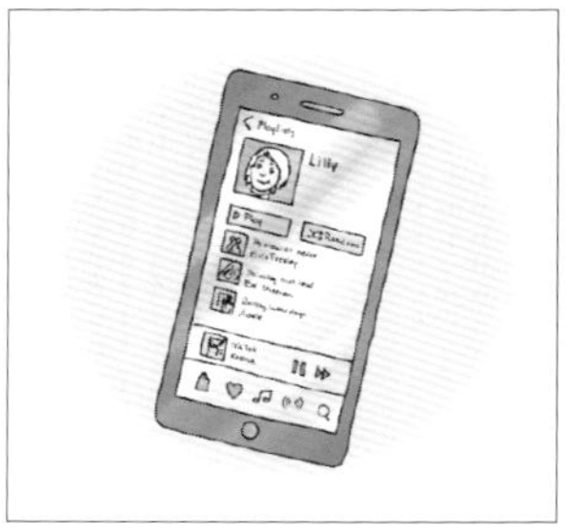

B ☐

C ☐

Part 2 – Questions 8–13: After the school lockdown

6 Punkte

Listen to the following conversation between Grace, a 15-year-old high school student from Bristol, and her grandmother. Grace is talking about her experiences with distance learning during the COVID-19 school lockdown.
For questions 8–13 tick (✓) the correct box A, B or C.
The first question is an example.

Example

0. Grace talks to …
   - A Mrs. Tomlinson. ☐
   - B her grandmother. ☑
   - C her sister Emma. ☐

8. For Grace the worst thing during the school lockdown was …
   - A wearing a mask. ☐
   - B not going to school. ☐
   - C not seeing her friends. ☐

9. After returning to school …
   - A they have to wear face masks. ☐
   - B not a lot has changed. ☐
   - C the students do a lot of group work. ☐

10. During the lockdown, Grace …
   - A spent less time on the computer than before. ☐
   - B was sometimes happy to turn off the screen. ☐
   - C became a screen addict. ☐

11. Grace preferred ...
   - A filling out worksheets as usual. ☐
   - B getting work back and correcting the mistakes. ☐
   - C working at her own speed. ☐

12. Grace really enjoyed ...
   - A the virtual forest walk with her biology teacher. ☐
   - B taking pictures of plants and insects. ☐
   - C talking to a nature guide about plants and insects. ☐

13. Emma freaked out because she ...
   - A got her mobile phone earlier than Grace. ☐
   - B deleted her work one day. ☐
   - C had to do online work. ☐

Part 3 – Questions 14–21: Mushroom coconut noodles

8 Punkte

Listen to this cooking podcast. Ella is going to describe how she prepares mushroom coconut noodles. For questions 14–21, fill in the gaps to complete the notes. The first question is an example.

This podcast is an episode of	0. Ella cooks easy food.
First you slice	14. ____________ mushrooms.
Mushrooms will be soft after	15. ____________
To make it yummy add	16. ____________ and
	17. ____________
For sweetness, add	18. ____________
Ella thinks the dish is the perfect	19. ____________
Another vegetable Ella suggests is	20. ____________
Preparation time	21. ____________

Part 4 – Questions 22–27: Why Germany is a great place to live

6 Punkte

You will hear a radio interview with Noah Clarkson, an American teenager who has just returned from a year in Germany as an exchange student.
For questions 22–27 decide whether each sentence is true or false.
Put a tick (✓) in the correct box 'true' or 'false'.
The first question is an example.

		true	false
Example	0. Emily Sanders spent a year in Germany.	☐	☑
	22. Noah's great-grandfather moved from America to Germany.	☐	☐
	23. Noah says that there is good public transportation in the US.	☐	☐
	24. Traveling on a bus in Germany is a practical way to get around.	☐	☐
	25. Noah traveled to other cities in Europe.	☐	☐
	26. In Germany people prefer traditional food to international food.	☐	☐
	27. Noah is going to Germany this summer.	☐	☐

II. Reading

Part 1 – Questions 1–7

Read the texts below. Then read the statements (1–7).
Decide whether the statements are true or false. Then tick (✓) the correct box.

7 Punkte

1.

Lost – Help me find my blue Fiat Panda 1.2

I have lost my blue Fiat Panda. I ran out of petrol and parked it on the side of the road. Stupidly I did not make a note of the road name.

If anyone spots a blue **FIAT PANDA**, **Registration KS63 VFW**, I would be very grateful for a hint.
A taxi picked me up at the bottom of the road and it was about a 30-minute drive back to Kingston where I live.

Contact JOHN 079417598348

2.

Cooking Class

Sign up for this free cooking class. You will learn how to shop for healthy meals and prepare them.

Cooking classes offer:

- Delicious recipes
- Cooking supplies
- Shopping tips

Sign up information:
Dates: Wednesday, Jan. 15, Feb. 19, Mar. 18
Time: 5 - 6:30 pm
Location: Family Health Center
Classes taught in English and Spanish
Interested?
Call 847-666-2425

3.

4.

SHOP SAFELY
AT YOUR FARMERS MARKET!

Help us practice safe and healthy shopping for all during the COVID-19 Pandemic.

NO CONTACT

- pay by card or use exact change if possible
- put your shopping into shopping bags yourself

HANDWASHING

- use hand washing stations before entering the market
- wash your hands regularly while shopping

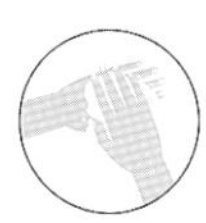

THANK YOU FOR YOUR HELP!

		true	false
1.	You must speak Spanish to join the cooking class.	☐	☐
2.	At the Farmers Market they will put your shopping into bags for you.	☐	☐
3.	John can't remember where he parked his car.	☐	☐
4.	In the literature class for young adults they will also show films.	☐	☐
5.	You can wash your hands before you enter the Farmers Market.	☐	☐
6.	John's car is parked about 30 minutes away from where he lives.	☐	☐
7.	You must bring your own cooking supplies.	☐	☐

Part 2 – Questions 8–14: 7 ways to minimize your carbon footprint

7 Punkte

Seven young people are speaking about ways they found to minimize their carbon footprint. For speakers 8–14 choose the correct statement A–I.
Write the correct letter (A–I) in the box next to the number. There are more statements than speakers. Each letter can only be used once.

A Find "greener" ways to get around.
B Take your own bag with you when shopping.
C Change the way you consume.
D Consume less meat.
E Plant more trees.
F Say no to plastic water bottles.
G Travel wisely – fly less.
H Unplug any electronics you're not using.
I Reduce water use.

8. ☐

Rita: My mum used to bring back loads of plastic bags whenever she went shopping. A few months ago, we decided to take our own shopping basket or bag with us when we go to the shops. The few times we forgot that and had to use a plastic bag, we at least made sure we reused it several times before we used it as a bin liner.

9. ☐

Ben: I have gone vegan. Did you know that it takes over 5 000 gallons of water to produce a single pound of beef? And that cows and sheep produce a lot of methane gas, which has a massive impact on global warming? I mean, not eating any meat was difficult but there are so many nice alternatives. You could start with a single vegan day, maybe a "Meatless Monday".

10. ☐

Annie: Whenever possible, unplug your electronic devices – TVs, computers or mobile phones because even when they're switched off, or all charged up, they're consuming energy. And since electricity production accounts for over 37 % of carbon dioxide emissions in the United States, unplugging is the way to go.

11. ☐

Joan: You hear it all the time "Plastic is bad!". Loads of the stuff ends up in landfills or even in the ocean where animals are badly affected by it. There are ways to use less plastic – I invested in a reusable water bottle and always carry it with me. There are many other things that are made from plastic and can easily be replaced by more sustainable alternatives.

12. ☐  **Harry:** I just got my driver's licence. But I am still not taking the car to go to school. Taking the bus or cycling is fine for me. I try not to use the car so much because how you get from A to B has a significant environmental impact. Walking, biking or taking public transport are all better than driving your car.

13. ☐  **Bob:** Buy fewer things and consume less. Recycle wherever possible, or reuse things. If you buy, buy high-quality things and make them last. You don't always need the latest mobile, try to use yours as long as possible or sell it on. It's important to save resources this way to reduce the impact on your carbon footprint.

14. ☐  **Sandra:** Don't let your water consumption run out of control! You can save up to 60 liters of water every week by turning off your tap while you brush your teeth. Every minute you spend in a shower uses up to 17 liters of water. Also, washing a full machine of clothes uses less water and energy than two half loads.

Part 3 – Questions 15–21: Fake News

For questions 15–21 tick (✓) the correct box true or false and give the line(s) where you find the information. You will only get a point if both parts of the answer are correct. 7 Punkte

Fake News

When you are online, you often see unwanted pictures, articles, links and videos trying to tell you their story. Often these stories are not true even though they sound and look like they could be. They have been specifically written to catch your interest and make you click on a story or an ad on another website. And sometimes those stories even tell lies to upset people for political reasons. This kind of news stories circulates quickly, and the result is fake news. Read these experts' tips to know when news is fake news and don't get fooled!

First of all, check the source: Look at the website where you found the story. Does it look real? Is the text well-written? Fake news websites often use web addresses (URL) that sound like real newspapers, but don't have many real stories about other topics.

Second, you should watch out for fake photos. Many fake news stories use photoshopped images. Sometimes, if you look closely at an image, you can see that it has been changed. So be careful and check the pictures.

Check if the story you are reading is on other news sites, too. If you find it on a number of other sites, then it probably isn't fake. Also find out about the website's sources. Serious news organizations check their sources before they publish a story.

Obviously, there are other signs for fake news. There are many techniques that fake news uses. For example, using ALL CAPS (and lots of ads that pop up when you click on a link). Also, think about how the story makes you feel. If the news story makes you angry, it's probably designed to do so.
If you know these things about online news, and use them in your everyday life, then you have control over what to read, what to believe and most importantly what to share. If you find a news story that you know is fake: don't share it!

How to spot fake news, https://learnenglish.britishcouncil.org/skills/reading/intermediate-b1/how-to-spot-fake-news

		true	false	line(s)
0.	This article is about fake news.	☑	☐	1
15.	Fake news looks like real news.	☐	☐	______
16.	Fake news is designed to get your attention.	☐	☐	______
17.	It's important to find out where the story comes from.	☐	☐	______
18.	Fake news websites always use original photos.	☐	☐	______
19.	You can find the same fake news on many different news sites.	☐	☐	______
20.	Some stories want to make you angry.	☐	☐	______
21.	You shouldn't send fake news to other people.	☐	☐	______

Part 4 – Questions 22–28: The story of fish and chips

7 Punkte

Read the following article about the history of fish and chips. Match the first parts of the sentences (22–28) with the sentence endings (A–I). There are more sentence endings than you need.

Long before the Big Mac was invented, Britain had its own national form of fast food.
"When I was a young man, it was great to have fish and chips once or twice a week," remembers 82-year-old Arthur Mowbrey. "Sixty years ago, you'd get a full-size portion of cod and chips for only a few pennies. It was cheap, and good. Every town in Britain had its fish'n'chip shops."
For a hundred years, they were the classic popular take-aways, British style. You could eat fish and chips in the street on your way home from work, or during the lunchbreak. Wrapped in newspaper, it would keep warm. Fresh sea fish could easily be bought in many British towns because they are near a port. Cheaper than meat, sea fish became a popular source of protein.
Things have changed. "Today young people prefer hamburgers or other take-away," says Lizzie, a teenager. "Fish'n'chips is a bit old-fashioned. But there are still cheap chip shops around. We sometimes have it at home, and we go and get it from the chip shop. It saves cooking!"

Thousands of chip shops have closed in the last twenty-five years. Some shops have survived in seaside towns, where the fish is really fresh. Traditionally, people visit them and eat there. Fish'n'chips wrapped in newspaper is already just a memory of the past. British and European hygiene rules no longer allow food to be wrapped in old papers, so today's carry-out chip shops use new paper or plastic boxes.
Fish and chips will survive as a specialty. Comfortable, more expensive fish restaurants with tables and chairs have existed for a long time. In the years to come, they may be the only type of fish'n'chip restaurant around.

No more fish'n'chips?, https://linguapress.com/intermediate/fish-chips.htm

		A	you don't have to cook.
22.	Many years ago, fish and chips	B	had fish and chips every week.
23.	When he was a young man, Arthur Mowbrey	C	eat fish and chips in restaurants where they can sit down.
24.	Fish and chips	D	were wrapped in a newspaper.
25.	Sea fish, a popular source of protein,	E	you can buy really fresh fish.
26.	In towns on the coast	F	invented the Big Mac.
27.	If you buy take-away fish and chips	G	keep you warm.
28.	In the future people will	H	is a typical British fast food.
		I	used to cost less than meat.

22.	23.	24.	25.	26.	27.	28.

III. Writing – Set I

Part 1 – AppWhats photo message: Summer holidays in Australia

10 Punkte

You are on holiday in Australia and send this picture to your friend Marc. He wants to know more about your holiday.

Great picture, huh?
Greetings from Australia!
Having a great time here!
See you soon!

Marc: Thank you! Are you there on holiday? Who is with you?

You: ______________________

Marc: How was your flight?

You: ______________________

Marc: What cool animals have you seen so far?

You: ______________________

Marc: What places have you been to? What else do you want to see?

You: ______________________

Marc: Have you planned any cool activities?

You: ______________________

Marc: And where are you staying?

You: ______________________

Marc: When will you be back? Can we meet up? I would love to see more pictures!

You: ______________________

Part 2 – Write a comment: Voluntary work

15 Punkte

Helping at an animal shelter, working for the fire brigade or supporting a social or ecological project at school – spend your free time working for a good cause! Become a volunteer!

Can you imagine spending your free time with voluntary work?

Give
- two pros,
- two cons,
- and your opinion. (Give reasons.)

Write about **80 words**.

III. Writing – Set II

Part 1 – Questionnaire: Smartphones in school

10 Punkte

You are spending a year abroad in London. Your school wants to allow students to use their smartphones in school. Help them to organise it by filling in the questionnaire.

Smartphones in school

How could you use your smartphone as an additional tool in class? Give two examples.

- ________________________________
- ________________________________

Would you like to use your phone during breaks? Give two reasons.

☐ Yes ☐ No

- ________________________________
- ________________________________

Name two disadvantages of using your phone in school and explain them.

- ________________________________
- ________________________________

Should there be a mobile-free zone in school? Say where and why or why not.

____

____

Give two rules for using the smartphone in school safely.

- ________________________________
- ________________________________

Part 2: Creative writing: The cave

15 Punkte

I was standing in front of the cave's entrance. Around the cave there were several different signs warning people to keep out. I wondered what could be in there. I had a torch, so ...

Complete the story.

Include the following aspects:
- what the signs said
- what was in the cave
- what happened next

Write about **80 words**.

Anhang – Hörverstehenstexte: G-Kurs

This is the listening part of the final examination 2021 levels A2 and A2 plus for schools in Lower Saxony.
There are four parts to the test. You will hear each part twice.
For each part of the test there will be time for you to look through the questions and time for you to check the answers. Write your answers on the paper. You must not speak during the test.

Part 1

Now look at part 1. There are 7 questions in this part. You will hear 7 short conversations. You will hear each conversation twice.
For each question there are three pictures and a short recording. Choose the correct picture and put a tick in the box below it.
Before we start, here is an example:

Part 1 – Example

Which tickets do they buy?

Man: While we're on the Internet, let's check which concert tickets we can get for Tim's birthday.
Woman: Oh, look here! Eminem's coming to town. His new album is fantastic, and the tickets aren't too expensive.
Man: Oh no, it's sold out already. But Taylor Swift is on tour too.
Woman: It's only you who likes her. Tim and I can't stand her! Tim prefers hip hop.
Man: What's this: Cro – hip hop from Germany. That sounds interesting.
Woman: I've heard about him. So, let's check it out.

The third picture is correct. So there is a tick in box C.

Part 1 – Text 1

Now look at the three pictures for question 1.
Now we are ready to start. Listen carefully. You will hear each recording twice.

When does the training take place?

Woman: Good morning, Brownton Swimming Pool.
Boy: Hello. I'd like some information about the water polo club.
Woman: Sure. We have an *Under 14 club*, an *Under 16 club* and an *Under 18 club*. How old are you?
Boy: I'm 15.
Woman: OK, so you want the *Under 16 club*.
Boy: When do they train?
Woman: Let's see – the under 16s train once a week on Tuesdays. No sorry – on Thursdays from 6:30 to 8 p.m. And matches are on Saturdays from 5:30 to 7:30 pm.

Boy: When does the training start?
Woman: Training starts next week.
Boy: Awesome. See you then.
Woman: OK, see you next week.

Now listen again.

Part 1 – Text 2

Which film do they want to watch?

Tamara: Hi, Mario, do you want to go and watch a film?
Mario: Hi, Tamara. Sure. What's on?
Tamara: There's a romantic comedy called *Forever*.
Mario: Hmm. I'm not sure. Are there any horror films on?
Tamara: Yes, there's *Midnight Moon*. It's got vampires in it.
Mario: OK. Sounds good. Let's go and watch *Midnight Moon*.
Tamara: Look, there's also a science fiction film, *Robot 2075*. What do you think?
Mario: Boring. No, I've already seen it.
Tamara: OK, let's meet at the cinema at seven.

Now listen again.

Part 1 – Text 3

Which main course do they order?

Waiter: What would you like to order?
Man: Hm, I'm not sure. I don't know whether to have the steak or the Thai chicken.
Woman: Be careful. The Thai chicken is very hot. Why don't you try the fish?
Man: I'm not keen on fish, but I like beef, so I'll go for the steak.
Woman: I'd like the Thai chicken and rice, please.
Waiter: Fine, great choice – and what would you like to drink?
Man: I'll have a fresh orange juice.
Woman: I'd like some mineral water, please.
Waiter: OK, thank you.

Now listen again.

Part 1 – Text 4

What problem does the man have?

Pharmacist: Hello, can I help?

Man: Yes, my wife sent me here because I can't stop coughing, it really hurts.

Pharmacist: Do you have a headache, too?

Man: Not really, no.

Pharmacist: Well, we have this syrup and this spray. The syrup is more expensive.

Man: Oh, well, I'll take the spray then.

Pharmacist: You know, you should really see a doctor if that cough continues or if you start having a temperature.

Man: Thanks, I'll do that.

Now listen again.

Part 1 – Text 5

Which road should you take into London?

Presenter: Traffic is crazy this morning. Here's an update for all drivers trying to get into London. There's heavy traffic on the motorways, including the M1 going south. You have to expect delays of at least an hour. Our advice is to get off the M1 and take the A41. The A1 is busy, too. It's not an alternative today. Have a safe trip!

Now listen again.

Part 1 – Text 6

At what time do the women meet?

Woman: Hi, Anna. Do you have a minute to talk about the meeting next Tuesday?

Anna: Sure, we said eleven, didn't we?

Woman: Yeah, we did. But I have a bit of a problem with the time. Would it be possible to move it?

Anna: Oh, I see. We could meet at one or sometime in the morning. What would be better for you?

Woman: Could we make it nine o'clock? That would really help me. I have another important meeting in the central office at twelve.

Now listen again.

Part 1 – Text 7

What kind of music will they have at their graduation party?

Boy: So, we still need to discuss the music for our graduation party. Last year they had a playlist with everybody's favorite music. I think that is the cheapest solution.

Girl: I have a better idea. My brother, he is in this cover band, and they'd love to have the chance to perform at our party.

Boy: A cover band? I'm not so sure. What about a DJ? Wouldn't that be more fun?

Girl: Yes, but a DJ is also very expensive. Do we have the money for that?

Boy: Hmm. Yes, we would have the money, but then we would have to cancel the catering. Would your brother's band charge anything?

Girl: No, I think they would play for food and drink.

Boy: Great. So that's decided then.

Now listen again.

This is the end of part 1.

Part 2

Now turn to part 2, questions 8 to 13. Listen to the following conversation between Grace, a 15-year-old high school student from Bristol, and her grandmother. Grace is talking about her experiences with distance learning during the Covid-19 school lockdown.
For questions 8 to 13, tick the correct box: A, B or C. The first question is an example.
You now have 30 seconds to look at part 2.
Now we are ready to start. Listen carefully. You will hear the recording twice.

Grandmother: So, are you back to school now?

Grace: Yes, we returned to school after the summer holidays. I am so happy to see all my friends again. I think that was the worst thing. Not having my friends around me for months on end.

Grandmother: And is school different now, or is it the same as before?

Grace: No, it's not really like before. The biggest change is that we have to wear our face masks in class. It gets really hot and stuffy, and we have to keep our distance to others, so we can't work in groups. But still, it's better than staying at home.

Grandmother: Why? I mean, you learned a lot when you stayed at home, didn't you? All that computer time you had?

Grace: Yes, my screen time was incredible. You know, I'm the screen addict in our family, and even I would say that my screen time has gone up a lot. I never thought I would say this, but some days I was happy when I could switch off the computer and wouldn't even touch my mobile for the rest of the day. You can get bored of technology after all.

Grandmother: When I remember my school time, it was all books and writing and exercise books and listening to the teacher. I can't really imagine what it was like to actually have lessons on the computer.

Grace: But it wasn't only lessons, it was so different. Some teachers sent us our work by email and we had to send it back when we finished. Then they gave us feedback and we had to correct things, but some teachers had some cool websites we could use for learning. We could do things at our own speed and got direct feedback from the website. That was cool.

Grandmother: But didn't I see you in a video chat some days? I thought that was school, too.

Grace: Yes, and that was the only chance I had to see some of my friends. Mrs. Tomlinson, my form teacher, always gave us some time for talking to our friends before or after the lessons. Then we did fun stuff in biology. One day she went for a walk in the forest and showed us live pictures of plants and insects and other interesting things. We followed her on our computer screens. We learned about the forest ecosystem, but this way it was more fun than just looking at pictures in the book.

Grandmother: So, you seem to have enjoyed it. And your sister, how did she cope?

Grace: Emma? Well, at first, she was happy because she's only ten years old and got that mobile phone two years earlier than I did. But she wasn't happy at all about all this online learning. She had never used the Internet for school projects before. She didn't know the software and had no clue about really using a computer for work. One day she freaked out because she deleted everything instead of saving her results. It was horrible. I wasn't there to help. Really sad.

Grandmother: Poor Emma. I hope she's doing better now. And you, enjoy school. Let's hope you don't have to go back to online learning any time soon.

Now listen again.

This is the end of part 2.

Part 3

Now turn to part 3, questions 14 to 21. Listen to this cooking podcast. Ella is going to describe how she prepares mushroom coconut noodles.
For questions 14 to 21 fill in the gaps to complete the notes. The first question is an example.
You now have 30 seconds to look at Part 3.
Now we are ready to start.
Listen carefully. You will hear the recording twice.

Ella: Welcome to another episode of *Ella cooks easy food.* Tonight, we have the ultimate Sunday night's supper. Creamy coconut milk peanut butter mushroom noodles. They're awesome. You got to make them. So, they're super, super easy. All you do is to slice up a pack of mushrooms and some spring onions. Then just boil some water to cook the noodles. And then we're going to fry the mushrooms with just a little bit of oil and salt and pepper. Let them get soft. That takes two minutes or so. Add a little bit of sesame oil.

It just adds a lovely flavor. Again, just let that cook for a minute. Now, we are going to make it yummy. Add about half a can of coconut milk and then two really generous teaspoons of peanut butter. The more peanut butter the better. And then you stir that in, and you'll see it getting really nice and thick and creamy. So, the mushrooms are really nice and soft now, and we're going to add the next bits. First, a little bit of lemon juice. I think the lemon juice just adds a bit of sweetness. That's quite nice. I just added half a lemon. You can add a little bit more at the end if you like. It's a perfect, quick Sunday night supper. All my friends love it. It's thick and creamy and the perfect comfort food. Now, just add a tiny bit of chili pepper, just a little sprinkle. But if you don't like hot spices, don't worry, leave it out. And you can add other vegetables to this as well as mushrooms. Some spinach in here would be really yummy as well. Just before you're about to finish, add your spring onions and let them cook for a minute or so and then it's ready. Mix the mushroom sauce with the noodles and serve it. So here it is, so creamy. Peanut butter coconut mushroom noodles, and I just couldn't recommend it more. It will only take you ten minutes. Just make it. Tell me what you think. Write your comments to ella@easyfood.com and make sure to come back next week for "Being chili".

Now listen to part 3 again.

This is the end of part 3.

Part 4

Now turn to part 4, questions 22 to 27. You will hear a radio interview with Noah Clarkson, an American teenager who has just returned from a year in Germany as an exchange student.
For questions 22 to 27 decide whether each sentence is true or false. Put a tick in the correct box: "true" or "false". The first question is an example.
You now have 30 seconds to look at part 4.
Now we are ready to start. Listen carefully, you will hear the recording twice.

Emily Sanders: Good morning, listeners. My name is Emily Sanders, and with me today is Noah Clarkson. He's 18 years old and he just returned from a year in Germany as an exchange student. Noah, why did you choose to go to Germany? And was it a good decision?

Noah Clarkson: Hey, thanks for having me on the show. Oh, it was the best decision of my life. Well, so far. I absolutely loved it in Germany and I'll definitely go back. I decided to go to Germany because my great-grandfather immigrated from there. So, I've always been curious what life is like there.

Emily Sanders: And what is it like? And what is it that you like about Germany?

Noah Clarkson: There are many things that Germany seems to do right and that make living awesome there. First, I love public transportation there. Here in the US, everyone uses their cars and there are hardly any buses or trains. In Germany, public transportation is such a good thing. You're able to skip the traffic and five or six minutes later, you're at your stop. And on the bus or the train, you can just relax. It's insane. It's super clean, super chill.

Emily Sanders: And obviously it's good for the environment. So, did you travel around a lot?

Noah Clarkson: Yeah, that's another cool thing. Germany is right in the middle of where you want to be in Europe. I traveled around a lot. You hop on a plane or train and within a few hours you're in another great place in Europe. For example, I went to Lisbon in two and a half hours or so. You're in another great country. You can use the same money and everything's so easy.

Emily Sanders: I see. What about the food? How did you like that in Germany?

Noah Clarkson: The food is awesome. There are lots of traditional German dishes, you know, sauerkraut, bratwurst and German potato salad. But most Germans don't actually eat that very often. They prefer Mediterranean, Italian or Turkish food. And it all tastes so awesome, so original. Here in America, most of the food is so greasy. In Germany, the food is healthier.

Emily Sanders: I'm sure you made some friends over there. Do you keep in touch?

Noah Clarkson: Yes. My host brother and a friend are coming to visit me over summer. I'm really looking forward to that.

Emily Sanders: Noah, thank you for sharing your impressions with us.

Now listen to part 4 again.

This is the end of the listening part. Good luck for the rest of your examination!

Abschlussarbeiten an der IGS in Niedersachsen
Englisch 2022

E-Kurs

I. Listening

Part 1 – Questions 1–7

7 Punkte

Listen to seven short recordings. For each recording, there is a question with three pictures. Choose the correct picture and put a tick (✓) in the box A, B *or* C *below it.*

Example

0. What is the man going to buy?

A ☐

B ☐

C ☑

1. Where does the band meet for the final rehearsal?

A ☐

B ☐

C ☐

2. Which dog is missing?

A ☐

B ☐

C ☐

3. When does the main boarding start?

A ☐

B ☐

C ☐

4. Where will the party be?

A ☐

B ☐

C ☐

5. What's the weather forecast for Friday?

A ☐

B ☐

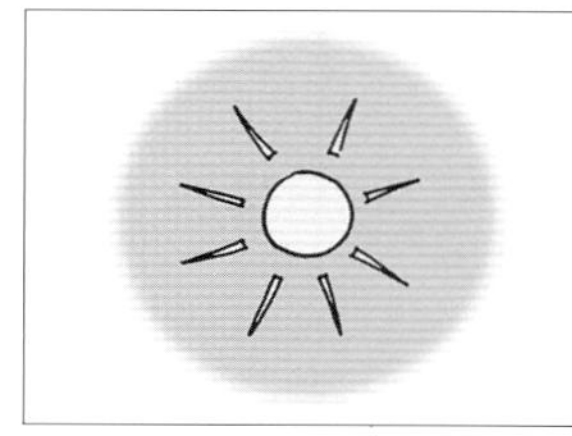

C ☐

6. How much flour are they adding to the pancake batter?

A ☐

B ☐

C ☐

7. Where is the couple going on holiday?

A ☐

B ☐

C ☐

Part 2 – Questions 8–13: Robin's New Life in New York City

Listen to Anne and Robin talking online about Robin's new life after he's moved from a small town in Oregon to New York City.
For each question, tick (✓) the correct box, a, b *or* c.

6 Punkte

8. Robin's new home ...
   a) has a backyard. ☐
   b) is near a skatepark. ☐
   c) is across the street from his school. ☐

9. At the moment, Robin mostly ...
   a) skates in the park. ☐
   b) explores New York City. ☐
   c) works on his basketball skills. ☐

10. Robin ...
    a) loves the skyscrapers and sights. ☐
    b) enjoys the atmosphere of the city. ☐
    c) thinks the city is too noisy for him. ☐

11. Robin's new school ...
    a) is smaller than his old school. ☐
    b) has a bad name in the city. ☐
    c) offers many activities. ☐

12. Rubio and Jalen have ...
    a) played basketball with Robin. ☐
    b) skated with Robin. ☐
    c) shown Robin around the city. ☐

13. Anne is going to visit Robin ...
    a) during spring break. ☐
    b) when school is out in June. ☐
    c) after her summer job. ☐

Part 3 – Questions 14–20: Staying at a Youth Hostel

7 Punkte

You are on a class trip in Copenhagen. The youth hostel manager tells you what you have to know about your stay. Fill in the missing information. The first question is an example.

Name of the youth hostel?	0. Danhostel Copenhagen
Location of students' and teachers' rooms?	14. ______
Where do I find my room number?	15. ______
Breakfast time and location?	16. ______
Who to inform in case of food allergies?	17. ______
Consequence of smoking?	18. ______
What should you do before going bowling?	19. ______
Wi-Fi password?	20. ______

Part 4 – Questions 21–26: Interview with an Influencer

6 Punkte

You will hear a radio interview with the social media influencer Emma D. Decide whether each statement is true or false and put a tick (✓) in the correct box. The first question is an example.

Emma D. …	true	false
0. is like most other influencers.	☐	✓
21. is sponsored by brands.	☐	☐
22. creates new outfits.	☐	☐
23. says that fashion trends repeat themselves.	☐	☐
24. says that her followers start buying lots of new clothes.	☐	☐
25. already sells her clothes online.	☐	☐
26. sells clothes for men and women.	☐	☐

II. Reading

Part 1 – Questions 1–6: Short Texts

Read the texts (1–6) below and read statements a, b *and* c *next to them. Decide which of the statements is the correct one for each text. Put a tick (✓) in the correct box next to the statement.*

6 Punkte

1. Today | 9:21 AM

Miriam! My mom promised we can have our sleepover this weekend. Try to convince your dad that you can come on Friday. Then you can stay for two nights. Wouldn't that be awesome?!

😀 XOXO Kaddy

a) Miriam is allowed to spend two nights at Kaddy's place. ☐

b) Kaddy would like Miriam to stay longer. ☐

c) Kaddy has to convince her mom. ☐

2.

Hey!

The bookshop phoned.

They've got the books you ordered but will only keep them till Thursday. Can you make it?

a) The books will be delivered to the shop on Thursday. ☐

b) The shop will order the books before Thursday. ☐

c) The books need to be collected by Thursday. ☐

3.

a) Cyclists must allow pedestrians to go first. ☐

b) Pedestrians must watch out for cyclists on this path. ☐

c) Cyclists must walk their bikes from here. ☐

4.

WAITER WANTED!

Standing on the front lines, our waiters are vital to the guest experience.
Can you handle such responsibility?

Our waiters should:

- Always be friendly and attentive.
- Be flexible. Working hours are not 9 to 5.
- Be experienced but it's no requirement.

a) People skills are most important for the job. ☐

b) People work regular hours. ☐

c) Work experience is necessary for the job. ☐

5.

a) Only elderly and physically challenged people may sit here. ☐

b) This seat has to be offered to elderly or physically challenged people. ☐

c) Elderly and physically challenged people will vacate this seat for you. ☐

6. Today | 7:21 AM

Hey Sam! Do you remember the backpack I had yesterday? I don't know where it is. Did I leave it in your flat? 🤞 It's not mine. I borrowed it and gotta give it back today! 😱 Thx, Bob

a) Bob has to return a backpack. ☐

b) Bob is looking for a backpack he can borrow. ☐

b) Bob left the flat with the backpack. ☐

Part 2 – Questions 7–13: An Interview with a Londoner

7 Punkte

Read the answers Alexa has given in an interview about her home town, London. On the next page there are eight questions. Decide which question is most suitable for each answer.
For texts 7–13 write the correct letter (A–H) in the box next to the number. There are more questions than answers. Each letter can only be used once.

7. ☐ I don't think there's a language that isn't spoken here. No matter where you come from, you fit right in. The city is one big melting pot of different cultures, languages and accents. At first, I thought it was British accents everywhere, but it turns out I was wrong.

8. ☐ People are always in a rush, so when they bump into you, they won't always apologize. I'm not criticizing Londoners because technically this doesn't mean that Londoners are rude. It just means that everyone has their own business to get to. They don't want to be late for their business meeting or class. Personally, if I were in a hurry in such a big, crowded city, I would do the same.

9. ☐ It is as appetizing as it sounds and looks. The best thing about it is: it's cheap! Usually, London is an expensive place to live, but it's a matter of where you go. Of course, right in the city where all the tourists go, you can't save any money. I enjoy some of the great Indian places in the suburbs.

10. ☐ It really depends on the neighbourhood. Theatres are a big thing – not just cinemas, but theatres where they produce plays. But the places people go to a lot are London's parks. They are huge! People go there to hang out with their friends, have a picnic, or just go outside and enjoy the weather. You can also find a gym at every corner, but they're expensive.

11. ☐ They say the weirder the better! You could walk into a fancy restaurant in pyjamas and they would still serve you. People start their own trends all the time. So, at one point, you just give up on trying to follow them. You begin to become more creative with your choices. Store-wise you find a lot of designer brands. That's why tourists think clothes are expensive here.

12. ☐ Like in most countries in the western world, the majority of the population is Christian. With London being so international, there is a lot more variety in religions than in most other cities in the world. Overall, London isn't much of a religious place but Christmas is a very big deal.

13. ☐ This may come as a surprise, but it isn't as big as it may seem in London. Sure, it's offered in some restaurants in the afternoon. And there are a couple of parlours that celebrate this British tradition. Actually, the amount of coffee shops found around this city is triple the number of tea parlours.

A How do Londoners spend their leisure time?

B Londoners are known for being polite. Is this true?

C How do you feel about the fashion in London?

D Would you say that London is an international city?

E How do Londoners usually get around?

F Is religion important in London?

G Is teatime still a thing there?

H What do you think of the food in London?

Adapted from: https://www.theteenmagazine.com/interviewing-a-londoner-what-it-s-like-to-live-in-london

Part 3 – Questions 14–19: Who is Banksy?

6 Punkte

Read the following article about the artist "Banksy".
For questions 14–19, tick (✓) the correct box, a, b *or* c.
For each question there is only one correct answer.

Every time a piece by Banksy appears people get very excited. His work can sell for over £ 1 million and is known all over the world.

But what do we really know about the mysterious artist? We don't exactly know who he is. Banksy is a famous – but anonymous – British graffiti artist. He keeps his identity a secret. It is assumed that he was born in Bristol around 1974. Although a lot of his art is produced in public places, he usually only reveals that it is his after it has appeared in his social media.

Banksy first got noticed for spray-painting trains and walls in his home city of Bristol during the early 1990s, before appearing in London. Street art and graffiti can be seen as criminal damage, so in the beginning it is thought the artist stayed anonymous to keep out of trouble. At first his pieces were mainly in Bristol, but in the 2000s his artworks started appearing all over the UK and other parts of the world.

A lot of his art is done in a particular style which people can easily recognise, because he chose to use a technique invented by the artist Blek le Rat to create his pieces: stencils – probably because it is a faster way to paint. However, Banksy does more than just street art: he has produced drawings, paintings and installation pieces. He even created his own theme park called Dismaland. Banksy's work is known for critical political messages, dealing with topics such as homelessness, racism or pollution.

Though regarded as mindless vandalism by some, the majority think his work is very valuable. As a result, his pieces can go for thousands of pounds.

Banksy has often made clear that he doesn't like to sell his work for so much money. In late 2018 *Girl with Balloon* (2006), a copy of one of Banksy's most popular wall paintings, partially destroyed itself with a hidden shredder at an auction just after being sold for $ 1.4 million. After that Banksy called the destroyed version *Love is in the Bin* and it was said to be the first work ever created

during a live auction. But its destruction most likely raised the value of the painting.
Since many people consider street art to be vandalism, some of his work was painted over as soon as it appeared. Sometimes graffiti artists put their own work over it. That's why the owner usually covers it up with plastic sheeting to protect it. There is a debate about why Banksy's work can be protected as 'art' when other graffiti artists are sometimes put in prison for doing the same thing

Adapted from: https://www.bbc.co.uk/newsround/51504255

14. We know …
    a) Banksy's real name. ☐
    b) that Banksy was born in Bristol. ☐
    c) that Banksy likes public places for painting. ☐

15. Banksy started his career …
    a) in the 2000s. ☐
    b) by spraying trains and walls. ☐
    c) in London. ☐

16. Banksy …
    a) creates street art called "Dismaland". ☐
    b) invented the stencil technique. ☐
    c) draws attention to political issues. ☐

17. Most people think that his art is …
    a) worth lots of money. ☐
    b) criminal damage. ☐
    c) pointless. ☐

18. Banksy's work "Girl with Balloon" …
    a) was sold just after its destruction. ☐
    b) probably lost value by its destruction. ☐
    c) was renamed after its destruction. ☐

19. Other street artists …
    a) have painted over Banksy's work. ☐
    b) protect Banksy's works with plastic covers. ☐
    c) criticise Banksy for vandalism. ☐

Part 4 – Questions 20–26: Long-Lost Sisters Find Each Other

7 Punkte

Read the article about two sisters, Victoria and Alyss. For questions 20–26, tick (✓) the correct box, true *or* false, *and give the line(s) of reference in the text. The first question is an example.*

27-year-old Victoria Voorhees knew she was adopted as a two-month-old girl. That's why she decided to take a WhoAmI-home DNA test to find out a bit more about her Hispanic background and genetic makeup.

She was astonished when the results revealed she had a sister and was sent a photo of a woman who looked very much like her.

As an adopted child, Victoria always dreamed of having an older sibling. But she couldn't believe her eyes when she first saw the photo of her sister. "At first, I was like: there's no way, that's impossible! Maybe they found someone that has some similarities to me? But I know now that's not how it works." She sent her sister a message through the WhoAmI-app and rushed home to tell her parents.

28-year-old Alyss Ravae and Victoria chatted. Then they joined a video call with their biological mother for the first time. "I showed her some photos of me growing up with my adoptive parents," says Victoria, "and she was happy but crying!"

Alyss says of her sister, "We live very parallel lives even though we were placed in very different situations."

It's not just their mutual love of Halloween, of Stephen King, of *It* and *The Shining* that she was fascinated by; they both have bat tattoos on opposite feet but the same part of the ankle.

Alyss said: "When she sent me that picture of her tattoo, I literally just dropped my phone." They also both have cats and make and sell pet portraits online.

Victoria said: "We both like hiking trails as well. I'm going to show her all the cool ones around here in Chicago!" To show everyone their similarities, the two sisters created a video for social media in which they demonstrate all the things they have in common. If you didn't know better, you'd think that these two people have spent all their lives together. Whereas in fact they have yet to meet in person. They are now planning to meet up for the first time as soon as possible.

Adapted from: https://www.goodnewsnetwork.org/sisters-long-lost-matching-tattoos-victoria-chicago

According to the article, Victoria …	true	false	line(s)
0. was adopted as a child.	☑	☐	1
20. took a test to learn about her genes.	☐	☐	____
21. never wanted any siblings.	☐	☐	____
22. sent a message to her parents.	☐	☐	____
23. also got to know her biological mother.	☐	☐	____
24. was shown photos of her sister growing up.	☐	☐	____
25. and her sister have lived in similar circumstances.	☐	☐	____
26. and her sister have shared their similarities with the rest of the world.	☐	☐	____

III. Writing – Set I

Part 1 – A Complaint: Empty Box

10 Punkte

You ordered a pair of Bluetooth earphones online but all you got was an empty box. Write a complaint to the online shop.

Include:

- *the reason for writing*
- *how you feel*
- *what you want the online shop to do*

Write about 80 words.

Part 2 – A Letter of Application: Au Pair Job

Inhalt: 7 Punkte
Sprache: 11 Punkte
Gesamt: 18 Punkte

You have found the following advert for an au pair job in Stockholm, Sweden, and decide to apply for it. Write about 150 words.

We are looking for an au pair that would enjoy spending time with our kids (boy and girl, aged 5 and 7), doing activities with them, speaking to them in English and fits in with the family.

Tell us about yourself:

- education, hobbies and interests
- work experience
- why you are the right person for this job

To: contact@aupair4u.com

Subject: Applying for an au pair job

III. Writing – Set II

Part 1 – A Comment: My Parents are Forcing Me into an Apprenticeship

You find the following post on a website and decide to leave a helpful comment. Write about 80 words. 10 Punkte

alex_06:

I'm just graduating from school and my parents are forcing me into an apprenticeship at their car dealership. I'd rather become a musician and don't care for cars at all. They say they're not going to support me in any other way. Can I make it without their support? What should I do?

97 reply share

Inhalt: 7 Punkte
Sprache: 11 Punkte
Gesamt: 18 Punkte

Part 2 – A Blog Entry: Time Travel into the Past

Imagine you had the chance to use a time machine and travel back in time for a day. Write a blog entry about that day.

In your text, include:

- *what time you decided to travel to and why*
- *what you experienced on that day*
- *whether or not you can imagine going back to that time again and explain why*

Write about 150 words.

Anhang – Hörverstehenstexte: E-Kurs

This is the listening part of the final examination 2022 level B 1 for schools in Lower Saxony. There are four parts to the test. You will hear each recording twice. For each part of the test there will be time for you to look through the questions. You must not speak during the test.

Part 1

Now look at part 1, questions 1 to 7. Listen to seven short recordings. For each recording, there is a question with three pictures. Choose the correct picture and put a tick in the box A, B or C below it. Before we start, here is an example.

Example

What is the man going to buy?

Man: I'm going shopping now. Anything else we need for our holiday?

Woman: The sunscreen from our last trip should still work. I haven't got any sunglasses, but I can borrow some of yours, can't I? Hm, maybe something to kill the time at the airport.

Man: Yes. That's a good idea. I'll stop by the newsagent's.

The picture with the magazine is correct. So there is a tick in box C.

Text 1

Look at the three pictures for question 1 now.
Now we are ready to start. Listen carefully.

Where does the band meet for the final rehearsal?

Principal: Good morning, staff and students of Hillary High School. Our school band is ready to play at the school festival next Saturday. The rehearsal this Tuesday will not be in the music room as usual due to groundworks. The band meets in the gym on Tuesday and on Friday they meet in the assembly hall for the final rehearsal. I'm looking forward to the festival and music from our great school band.

Now listen again.

Text 2

Which dog is missing?

Woman: This is Loved And Lost Animals' Home. How can I help you?

Man: Hello. My name is Jack Austen. Our dog, Leo, ran off yesterday morning. Maybe someone brought him in to you?

Woman: Let's see. Could you describe your dog, please?

Man: It's a crossbreed with black fur and a white head, long, hanging ears and a short tail. He wears a collar around his neck.

Woman: Right. I'll check for you. Can you call back in 10 minutes?
Man: Yes, of course. Thank you.

Now listen again.

Text 3

When does the main boarding start?

Announcer: Good morning to all passengers for Kansas City. This is the boarding announcement for flight AA3421 to Kansas City. Your boarding starts at 9.20. For passengers with young children, as well as passengers requiring special assistance, boarding starts at nine. Priority boarding starts at 9.10. Please have your boarding pass and identification ready. Thank you for your attention.

Now listen again.

Text 4

Where will the party be?

Girl: You know what? I didn't get Ben's invite, but he told me I could come to his party. It's on Saturday, right? But where is it? At his house?

Boy: Yeah, it's at his place. I think he wanted to celebrate down by the river, but that didn't work out for some reason. He thought about renting a club, but ... too expensive. And some folks would have been too young to get in.

Now listen again.

Text 5

What's the weather forecast for Friday?

Speaker: The weather forecast for this weekend doesn't look too promising, really. There's going to be some heavy rain and temperatures in the low sixties. If you're planning on having a barbecue, you might want to do that on Friday. It should still be dry. You shouldn't expect any sunshine, though.

Now listen again.

Text 6

How much flour are they adding to the pancake batter?

Boy: Okay, let's make pancakes. How much flour do we need?

Girl: The recipe says 200 grams, but I don't think that would be enough for the five of us.

Boy: That's true. Let's make it 300, then. That'll leave 700 grams for David's birthday cake on Saturday.

Girl: Brilliant. So let's add the eggs and the milk.

Now listen again.

Text 7

Where is the couple going on holiday?

Woman: Look, this website has some great holiday deals. You know, I've always wanted to go to a desert island.

Man: And I cannot think of anything more boring. How would you feel about going to the mountains? I believe it's not that hot there. Or how about going to a big city by the sea? Look, there's Rio and there's Sydney.

Woman: Cities are probably one of the hottest places of all. You know, I'd love to go hiking again.

Man: Me too. I think there's only one place where we can do that.

Now listen again.

This is the end of part 1.

Part 2

Now turn to part 2, questions 8 to 13. Listen to Anne and Robin talking online about Robin's new life after he's moved from a small town in Oregon to New York City. For each question, tick the correct box, a, b *or* c. *You now have 30 seconds to look at part two.*
Now we are ready to start. Listen carefully.

Anne: Hey, Robin, can you hear me?

Robin: Yeah. So nice to see you. How are you?

Anne: Good. How's life in New York?

Robin: It's crazy. You can't imagine.

Anne: Really? Hit me.

Robin: Well, we moved to the Upper West Side in Manhattan. So, we don't have our own house with a backyard anymore. Just an apartment. It felt kind of small at first, but now I got used to it. Cool thing is there's a skate park across the street and my new school is only two blocks away. So, no more endless bus rides twice a day.

Anne: A skate park. Nice. So, you still skate a lot?

Robin: Not really. I've just been there once so far. I haven't had the time to explore the city yet. I really want to get on the basketball team. Pretty much all I do is work on my shot. Tryouts are next week.

Anne: What? You're living in the most amazing city in the world and haven't even checked it out yet?

Robin: Well, of course, a little bit. This city is unbelievable. I mean, the skyscrapers and sights aren't bad, but it's the vibe of the city that really gets me. It's true what they say – this city never sleeps. There's always something going on in the streets. Everything's so loud here. It bothered me at first, but now I don't really notice it anymore.

Anne: Really? I don't know. I think I prefer the peace and quiet here in Oregon. So, how's school?

Robin: Everything is so different. Way bigger. Not like our tiny school back in Oregon, but still, the school has a good team spirit because there is a different assembly or team project every week. Also, it's supposed to be one of the better inner-city schools. You can choose classes that I had never heard of before. It's great.

Anne: That's nice. Have you met some cool people to hang out with?

Robin: Yeah, I met Rubio and Jalen on the basketball court in the park. Now we're practicing together for the tryouts, and they told me they also skate. After we've hopefully all made the team, they're going to show me all the nice spots to skate in the city.

Anne: Sounds nice. When am I going to meet them?

Robin: You want to come visit? That's great. Come right away!

Anne: Like New York's around the corner. But, yeah, I think I could come see you in spring break. Or wait, I'll come over in summer. We'll have much more time then. School's out in June, and I'll be counseling at a summer camp right after. But I'm free all of July and August.

Robin: Great. Book a flight. I can't wait to show you everything. Remember when I was so afraid of moving here? Now I really feel at home. You know, I definitely miss you guys, but we can always stay in touch and visit. So, tell me, what's up in T-Lake? Is Angie still with ...

Now listen again.

This is the end of part 2.

Part 3

Now turn to part 3, questions 14 to 20. You are on a class trip in Copenhagen. The youth hostel manager tells you what you have to know about your stay. Fill in the missing information. The first question is an example. You now have 20 seconds to look at part three.
Now we are ready to start. Listen carefully.

Hello, everybody. Please listen up. Welcome to Danhostel, Copenhagen. I'm Ola. I'm the hostel manager. I'd like to give you some useful information on your stay, so please note down the most important things. Your teacher told me he's going to test you later tonight. First, your rooms are on the second floor, and your teachers' rooms are on the first floor. The rooms are right below yours, so your teachers are closer than you might think. You'd better watch out. You will all get one of these key cards. You can find your room numbers on them so that you don't accidentally knock on the wrong doors. Make sure you don't lose your card, as there is a € 10 deposit on it. I guess you'd like to get that back at the end of your stay. Breakfast is served on the top floor from 7 to 10. You can eat as much as you like, but do not smuggle anything out. If you want to get some supplies for your trips, you can buy a lunch bag for € 3 at the entrance to the dining hall. Dinner is from 6 to 8. You can choose between two different meals. Vegan and vegetarian. If you eat nothing but meat, you will go hungry. We are a meatless hostel. Please let the kitchen staff know if you're suffering from any intolerances or food allergies. Our chefs will be happy to provide you with tasty alternatives. For example, we offer some excellent

gluten-free specials. In case you are still hungry at night, there's a snack machine on each floor. The quiet time starts at 11. That's when you have to stay in your rooms and also turn down the volume. Alcoholic drinks, smoking or other drugs are strictly prohibited. If you break this rule, you will be expelled immediately.
If you get bored in the evening, you can use the bowling alley in the basement. We've got six lanes. If you don't only want to watch other people bowl but have a go yourself, you should make a reservation in advance. Bowling is extremely popular at the moment. Maybe that's because it's free. The shoes, however, are not. The rent is € 5 for a pair, and you're not allowed to bowl without them. On departure day, make sure to clean your room. Remove the sheets from your bed and put them into the laundry container, which you will find on your floor on the day of your departure. Now enjoy your stay. And if you have any questions, let me know. All right. The Wi-Fi password: DHC – all in capital letters – 2022 – in numbers. So DHC2022. Have a great stay.

Now listen again.

This is the end of part 3.

Part 4

Now turn to part 4, questions 21 to 26. You will hear a radio interview with the social media influencer Emma D. Decide whether each statement is true or false and put a tick in the correct box. The first question is an example. You now have 30 seconds to look at part four.
Now we are ready to start. Listen carefully. You will hear the recording twice.

Radio host: Good morning, listeners. With me today is a person some of you might already know. If so, you've come across her photos and stories on Instapic. Her name is Emma D., and you can find her under her username at Emma – underscore – D. And perhaps you've noticed that she's unlike most other influencers. Hi, Emma. It's a pleasure to have you on the program today.

Emma: Good morning. Thanks for having me.

Radio host: For those who don't know you, what do you do differently than most other influencers out there?

Emma: Well, most other influencers are sponsored by brands. It's their job to promote their products, the latest fashion, the newest makeup, the coolest technology and all the stuff that people care about. I, on the other hand, like used clothes and accessories and want to show what you can do with them. For example, followers send me clothes they don't wear anymore, and I turn them into new outfits and post them on my site.

Radio host: I happen to be one of your followers, and I have to admit, it's really hard to believe that it's all second hand. What inspired you to completely focus on second hand?

Emma: The thing is trends are never completely new. Big sunglasses – that was a trend in the eighties and now people are wearing them again. So why buy new ones if it's all been there before? Many people throw their stuff away because they think it's not fashionable anymore. I think that's idiotic. I followed other influencers and thought that they're not sending the right message. We live in a throwaway society, and I really don't like that.

Radio host: I absolutely agree. What do you think: how did you become so successful and gain so many followers?

Emma: I think many people have realized that if we continue living the way we do at the moment, we will need more than one planet. Things have to change, and people know it. And it's a fact: following the latest trends and buying loads of new clothes is not something that makes you happy in the long run. It only satisfies you for a short while. But I show my followers how to be creative and make a lot out of a little, and they tell me that they find it inspiring. They begin to appreciate the things that they already have. It actually makes them happy, and that makes me happy in return. And last but not least, they're saving a lot of money.

Radio host: That's an interesting point. But speaking of money, can you actually make a living off of it?

Emma: Well, I can't live from my postings, but that's not my goal. I'm running a local second-hand shop. Many of my followers go there to buy what they see online or trade in their old clothes. Also, I want to start selling these clothes online too – at fair prices, of course.

Radio host: So, you're using and reselling clothes for women only?

Emma: Well, most of my followers and customers are women, but most clothes can be worn by men and women. It's just a matter of how you want to design your outfit. There's nothing gender-specific in what I do.

Radio host: Emma D., thank you for sharing your thoughts with us. I hope your ideas go viral and other influencers start listening and trying to make the world a better place, too. Coming up in our program is Stephen, who reads out children's books online. Stay tuned.

Now listen again.

This is the end of the listening part. Good luck for the rest of your examination!

G-Kurs

I. Listening

Part 1: Questions 1–6

6 Punkte

You will hear six short conversations.
You will hear each conversation twice.
For each question there are three pictures and a short recording.
Choose the correct picture and put a tick (✓) in the box below it.

0. Which tickets do they buy?

Example

A ☐ B ☐ C ☑

1. What activity would Sally prefer?

A ☐ B ☐ C ☐

2. Which extra activity does Paula choose?

A ☐ B ☐ C ☐

3. What does Martha buy?

A ☐

B ☐

C ☐

4. What will Marc do next?

A ☐

B ☐

C ☐

5. What present will Peter buy for Sally's birthday?

A ☐

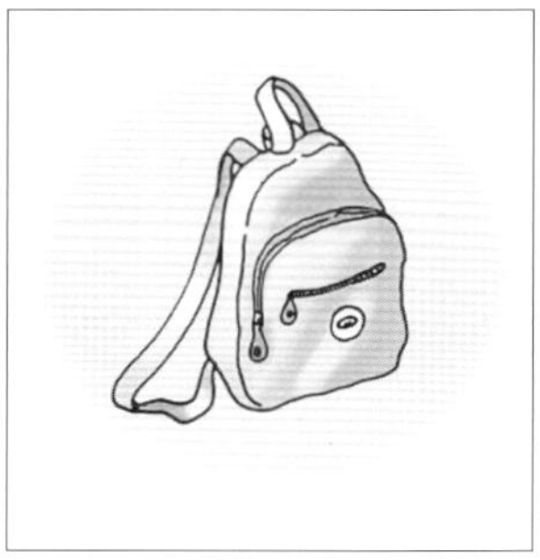

B ☐

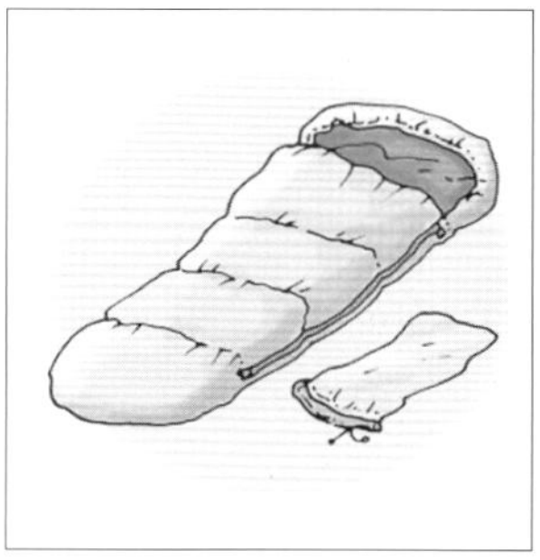

C ☐

6. What pet will the family get?

A ☐

B ☐

C ☐

Part 2: Questions 7–13: A spooky hotel

7 Punkte

Listen to the following interview between Mrs. Moth and Fox Badger from the "z-files YouTube-Channel".
Mrs. Moth talks about a spooky experience in an old hotel in Scotland.
For questions 7–13 tick (✓) the correct box A, B or C.
The first question is an example.

0. Mrs. Moth gives an interview for …
   - A a magazine. ☐
   - B social media. ☑
   - C a TV show. ☐

7. Mrs. Moth and her husband …
   - A have been to Edinburgh several times. ☐
   - B were in Edinburgh for the first time last year. ☐
   - C went to Edinburgh last month. ☐

8. The hotel was …
   - A in an old castle built 750 years ago. ☐
   - B in an old house built in about 1750. ☐
   - C at 750 Edinburgh Street. ☐

9. When the lights went off Mrs. Moth heard …
   - A someone breathing. ☐
   - B her husband speaking. ☐
   - C the sound from the TV. ☐

10. At first, she thought …
    - A someone was making a joke. ☐
    - B her husband had switched off the light. ☐
    - C the sound was coming from the wardrobe. ☐

11. She saw the ghost …
    - A standing next to her husband. ☐
    - B in the darkness. ☐
    - C after the light came on. ☐

12. The hotel manager told them that …
    - A they were the first people to see the ghost. ☐
    - B other people had seen the ghost before. ☐
    - C the owner of the house first saw the ghost. ☐

13. They …
    - A couldn't sleep in their room. ☐
    - B had to stay in their room. ☐
    - C checked into another room. ☐

Part 3: Questions 14–21: Monmouth's got Talent

8 Punkte

Listen to this announcement for a talent show. It tells you what the talent show is and how you can enter. For questions 14–21, fill in the gaps to complete the notes. The first question is an example.

The popular student event is called	0. Monmouth's got Talent.
This year the event is	14. ______
Britain's got Talent is a BBC	15. ______
One talent the speaker mentions is	16. ______
This event presents talents from all	17. ______
Money will be raised for a network of	18. ______
Send your entry videos to	19. ______
The winners will be presented on YouTube on	20. ______
The winner will get	21. ______

Part 4: Questions 22–28: An interview with a musician

7 Punkte

You will hear an interview with Andy Keating, the guitar player of the band IST IST from Manchester. He talks about the effects Covid 19 had on the music industry in greater Manchester. For questions 22–28 decide whether each sentence is true or false. Put a tick (✓) in the correct box 'true' or 'false'. The first question is an example.

		true	false
0.	Andy Keating is the guitar player of the band IST IST.	✓	☐
22.	He is talking about the music business during Covid.	☐	☐
23.	The tickets for the planned concerts were sold out.	☐	☐
24.	Some musicians had to work in other businesses.	☐	☐
25.	Keating says that Covid has not changed the Manchester music scene.	☐	☐
26.	When you want to go to a concert you will have to do a quick Covid test.	☐	☐
27.	The DJ hopes there will soon be cultural events in Manchester again.	☐	☐
28.	IST IST are planning a world tour after the summer.	☐	☐

II. Reading

Part 1: Questions 1–6

Read the texts below. Then read the statements (1–6).
Decide whether the statements are true or false. Then tick (✓) the correct box. 6 Punkte

1.

TEACHING YOU TO BECOME THE PACK LEADER

Fully qualified with 20 years' experience in training Security and Police Protection dogs.

Group training classes on
Wednesday 11 am
Friday 10 am
Saturday 11 am

I offer one-on-one sessions and group training sessions.

HOME BOARDING
Looking after your dogs in my own home if you're going away, where training can be provided if needed with cats, chickens or even other dogs.

Email
dogrehab@gmail.com for more info

First-time clients receive 10% off!

2.

Bad Art Night: https://www.metrolibrary.org/events/bad-art-night (adapted)

3.

Vegan Baking Class

No dairy, no eggs? No problem!

Our vegan chefs will introduce you to some wonderful vegan ingredients and help you in your quest to master vegan baking.

From nutty chocolate cookies to sticky toffee puddings, we'll inspire your vegan self in this 2-hour online baking session.

This class is fun, relaxed and eggless!

Call us for more information:
01514563219
To take part, register by mail:
info@veganbaking.com

4.

Hamilton Pool Preserve

Hamilton Pool Preserve is a historic swimming hole with a natural 50 ft waterfall near Austin/Texas. The waterfall never completely dries up. The preserve is home to a variety of native birds, fish, animals and plants.

Reservations are required to visit. Swimming is not guaranteed.

Additional information:
- Pets are not allowed
- Quarter-mile hike on rough terrain
- Reservations are for up to 8 people and one vehicle

	true	false
1. You must write an email to sign up for the Bad Art Night.	☐	☐
2. At the Bad Art Night, you will use old things to create a piece of art.	☐	☐
3. At Hamilton Pool Preserve you can park next to the waterfall.	☐	☐
4. For the dog training you can choose between individual or group sessions.	☐	☐

		true	false
5.	You can take part in the baking class from home.	☐	☐
6.	You can bring your dog to Hamilton Pool Preserve.	☐	☐

Part 2: Questions 7–13: Fancy restaurants

7 Punkte

Read these people's statements about the food they like and the short descriptions of various types of restaurants. Decide which restaurant (7–13) is most suitable for which speaker (A–I). There are two more speakers than restaurants. Write the correct letter (A–I) in the box next to the number. Each letter can only be used once.

A "My girlfriend loves Italian food, especially fresh pasta. I am looking for a romantic spot for a special occasion!" *John, aged 22*

B "I have got quite a short lunch break. Where can I get something decent to eat with good value for money?" *Melissa, aged 27*

C "We like to enjoy dinner, but our kids love to play when they finished their meals. So, we definitely need a place with a playground." *Bob, aged 32*

D "I love eating pizza, pasta and lovely desserts. But because I'm strictly vegan, a restaurant is hard to find." *Chloe, aged 20*

E "My friend has a sweet tooth and I want to take her somewhere special this weekend." *Lucy, aged 16*

F "I really like spicy food. Can you recommend somewhere good in town? I might go to a club afterwards." *Dino, aged 21*

G "At the weekends I like to start with the most important meal of the day. Do you know a place that serves a hearty breakfast and a tasty cappuccino?" *Micky, aged 31*

H "My boyfriend and I love eating fish. But he's not a big fan of quiet restaurants. He likes entertainment." *Caroline, aged 19*

I "My girlfriend and I are vegetarian. Can you recommend a suitable restaurant for a healthy lunchtime meal with a delicious sweet treat afterwards?" *Tom, aged 18*

Adapted from: https://learnenglishteens.britishcouncil.org/skills/reading/intermediate-b1-reading/food-restaurants

7. ☐ Looking for a restaurant right in the city centre and a perfect location before going on a night out? In this case, *MahaRaja* is the right choice for you. Our specialty is various traditional chicken dishes. But it's not always the meat that matters. Our veggie food is also really "hot". For authentic Indian taste there is extra hot.

8. ☐ No matter if you are into elegant dining in a stylish atmosphere for a special evening or if you prefer a delicious lunch in a relaxed setting, *Bella* is the place to go. Our chefs know how to make tasty traditional pasta. Every Friday there is a special Italian night with a great pasta and seafood buffet.

9. ☐ This is the ideal place for people who love sausages, baked beans, bacon and eggs, toast and marmalade for a good start to the day. In *The English*

Rose Cottage this is served with a strong cup of breakfast tea, or you can choose from a variety of different coffee specialities. Enjoy your full English brekki at any time during the day and listen to your favourite 1990s songs.

10. ☐ This charming restaurant serves organic food that's got taste! Come to the *Green Elephant* at lunchtime for our famous super-size burgers with "meat" made from plants. In the afternoon, go for a great fruit salad or enjoy a coffee and a delicious piece of cake. Regionally grown fruit and vegetables.

11. ☐ You haven't got bags of time but fancy traditional fish and chips or a really tasty hamburger made with the best meat? *Better Quick Bites* is a modern café where food – while served fast – is not junk food! Quality is particularly important here, and our prices are good, too.

12. ☐ *Sweet Treat* is the ideal place for people who are mad about chocolate and sweet snacks. We serve a variety of wonderful desserts, sweets and cakes. Chocolate lovers will be excited by our amazing range of chocolate cakes.

13. ☐ Come inside *Soul Food* and let the good times roll! Our new restaurant has different types of live music every night except Mondays, and excellent food that is cooked with the finest ingredients. There are great fish dishes but also steak and pizza. Join us on Friday nights for the best soul music in town!

Part 3: Questions 14–20: 3 Things I Learned after a 31 Day Social Media Break

Read this article about a young woman who didn't use social media for a month. For questions 14–20 tick (✓) the correct box <u>true</u> or <u>false</u> and <u>give the line(s) where you find the information</u>. You will only get a point if both parts of the answer are correct.

7 Punkte

One month ago, I decided I was going to quit social media for one month. So I deleted Snapchat, Instagram, and TikTok.

I spent around 4 hours a day on social media, and when you multiply that by 31 days, I was spending *124 hours a month* on social media.

So, I knew that I needed some time off. Now, one month later, I want to describe three of the biggest benefits I received from living life, social media-free.

Improving relationships is probably the most obvious benefit. With my phone, I would check my crush's Snapchat or "stalk" my friends' Instagrams. When I wasn't able to do those things, I instantly felt that my relationships became stronger. Since I could only communicate in-person with people, I found myself valuing the time I spent with them more, and I was even able to find out new things about them.

Learning to love myself was the second benefit. A lot of times, I scrolled through a model or influencer's profile, always comparing my appearance to theirs and trying to be as perfect as they seemed to be. But, without social media, I stopped that and became more confident.

And – last but not least – I stopped being so lazy. One month ago, the first thing I would do after school was sit on the couch and open my phone up to the TikTok "For You" page. Once I got to studying, I still would take long breaks to scroll through my phone. Then, I would have to rush on all my assignments. Today I start my homework as soon as I get home and end up with hours of free time afterwards.

You might have realized now that you have a social media problem, just like I did. So do something about it!

It doesn't have to be as extreme as completely deleting everything: instead, you could set limits on your screen time, or you could make it fun by competing with friends to see who can last the longest without social media. After all, what do you have to lose?

Adapted from: https://www.theteenmagazine.com/3-things-i-learned-after-a-31-day-social-media-detox

	true	false	line(s)
0. The author decided to take a social media break.	☑	☐	1
14. The author used to spend more than 120 hours online each month.	☐	☐	______
15. The author wants to show the good sides of a social media break.	☐	☐	______
16. The author says it is difficult to keep up good relationships with friends without social media.	☐	☐	______
17. The author says you may get to know your friends even better without social media.	☐	☐	______
18. The author thinks it's easier to accept yourself the way you are if you don't look at models or influencers.	☐	☐	______
19. Before her social media break the author used to spend a lot of time on her phone after finishing her homework.	☐	☐	______
20. The author says you must be very strict with yourself to benefit from a social media break.	☐	☐	______

Part 4: Questions 21 – 27: Croissant scare

7 Punkte

Read the following article about a funny event in Poland.
Match the first parts of the sentences (21–27) with the sentence endings (A–I).
There are more sentence endings than you need.

A lot of people are afraid of spiders, but have you ever heard of people being afraid of croissants?

Believe it or not, one of these traditional French sweet breakfast rolls scared many residents of the Polish city of Krakow. Elzbieta Wojcik, aged 76, looked out of her kitchen window last March and saw a strange brown object hanging in a tree. She thought it was a kind of dangerous animal and warned her neighbours. The residents were so worried that they kept their windows closed for a couple of days. In the end they called for help to get the "animal" removed from the tree opposite their apartment building.

Later, the Krakow Animal Welfare Society wrote on its Facebook account that a woman called the authorities to report an unidentified animal sitting in the tree. Animal welfare officers phoned the residents in the building and asked them to describe the animal. One resident explained that the animal looked like a large brown bird; another said it was a kind of lizard.

Although the inspectors knew that it was almost impossible that a reptile would survive the cool spring temperatures in the southern Polish city, they wondered if the animal could have been an unwanted pet thrown out by its owners.

The animal welfare officer explained what happened: He said he went to the apartment building where the residents lived to check on the strange animal. He reported that he spotted a "brown creature sitting on a tree branch," and that its "brown fur was shining in the sun". He then added: "The poor little thing had no legs or head." When he discovered that the strange beast was a croissant, probably thrown out of a window to feed the birds, he was "almost swept off his feet by a laughing attack".

"But", he said "Better safe than sorry!" The public should continue to be careful and report any sightings of strange animals.

Adapted from: https://breakingnewsenglish.com/2104/210418-croissant.html

		A	didn't open their windows for some days.
21.	People in Krakow were afraid	B	an unidentified animal.
22.	They were so afraid that they	C	would survive in cold weather.
23.	The woman told the authorities about	D	started laughing.
24.	One person described the thing as	E	of a croissant hanging in a tree.
25.	The officer first thought it	F	report unusual things.
26.	When the officer found out what the thing was, he	G	could be an unwanted pet.
27.	The authorities want people to	H	of feeding birds.
		I	a large brown bird.

21.	22.	23.	24.	25.	26.	27.

III. Writing: Set I

Part 1: AppWhats photo message: At the airport

10 Punkte

You are at the airport waiting for your flight and you send this picture to your friend Kevin. He wants to know more about your holiday plans.

Guess where I am.
I am so excited!

Kevin: Oh wow, you are at the airport! Where are you going?

You: ____

____

Kevin: Oh, I didn't know. **When** did you decide that and **why** are you going there?

You: ____

____

Kevin: Who's with you?

You: ____

____

Kevin: What do you plan to do there? **Which** places do you want to see?

You: ____

____

Kevin: Where are you staying?

You: ____

____

Kevin: How long will ycu stay? **When** will you be back?

You: ____

____

Kevin: Wow, I would love to see more pictures. Do you think we can meet after your trip?

You: ____

____

Part 2: Writing an article – One day without electricity

15 Punkte

Last Thursday there was no electricity and no internet in your village. Write an article for your school magazine about your day without electricity.

- *What was your first reaction?*
- *What was difficult?*
- *Which things didn't work and what did you use instead?*
- *How did you spend your day?*

Write about 80 words.

Words: ________

III. Writing: Set II

Part 1: Application form for a talent show

10 Punkte

You want to take part in a talent show. Before they invite you, you have to fill in this application form.

Application Form "Talent Show"

Name: ______________________ Date of birth: ______________________

Gender: ______________________ Email: ______________________

Describe your talent in detail. ______________________

____

What equipment do you need for your performance? ______________________

____

Tell us something about yourself. (hobbies, family …) ______________________

____

____

What would you do if you won the 500 Euro prize? ______________________

____

How long did it take you to practise your performance? ______________________

____

How did you find out about the contest? ______________________

____

Which two people would you like to invite? ______________________

____

Part 2: A short story: A box on the doorstep

15 Punkte

Read the beginning of the story and finish it.

Last night when he came home, he found a box on his doorstep. He hadn't ordered anything …

Write about 80 words.
Include the following ideas:

- *What was in the box?*
- *Who was it from?*
- *How did he feel?*
- *What happened next?*

Words: ___________

Anhang – Hörverstehenstexte: G-Kurs

This is the listening part of the final examination 2022 levels A2 and A2 plus for schools in Lower Saxony.
There are four parts to the test. You will hear each part twice.
For each part of the test there will be time for you to look through the questions and time for you to check the answers. Write your answers on the paper. You must not speak during the test.

Part 1

Now look at part 1. There are 7 questions in this part. You will hear 7 short conversations. You will hear each conversation twice. For each question there are three pictures and a short recording. Choose the correct picture and put a tick in the box below it. Before we start, here is an example:

Example

Which tickets do they buy?

Man: While we're on the Internet, let's check which concert tickets we can get for Tim's birthday.

Woman: Oh, look here! Eminem's coming to town. His new album is fantastic, and the tickets aren't too expensive.

Man: Oh no, it's sold out already. But Taylor Swift is on tour too.

Woman: It's only you who likes her. Tim and I can't stand her! Tim prefers hip hop.

Man: What's this: Cro – hip hop from Germany. That sounds interesting.

Woman: I've heard about him. So, let's check it out.

The third picture is correct. So there is a tick in box C.

Text 1

Now look at the three pictures for question 1.
Now we are ready to start. Listen carefully. You will hear each recording twice.

What activity would Sally prefer?

Sally: My cousin is coming to visit me next weekend. I don't know what I can do with him.

Boy: Why? The weather is nice and maybe you can take him canoeing on the river. You like canoeing, don't you?

Sally: Yes, I do. And I'd love to go. But he's not an active person. More the indoor type. He likes books and museums and computer games.

Boy: Hmm, difficult. The Science Museum has this special show about the Mars landing. Maybe you could go there, or you could play a computer game together.

Sally: I think I'll ask him what he prefers to do. Canoeing or the museum. I know what I would choose.

Now listen again.

Text 2

Which extra activity does Paula choose?

Henry: Hi, Paula. Have you already chosen your extra activity for next term?

Paula: It's so hard to decide. I love playing the guitar, so I thought about joining the school band. But I also like art. You know that I'm good at drawing, right?

Henry: Oh, yes. I love your drawings. I think you should do art, but wait, what about acting? You like playing different roles, don't you?

Paula: Oh, yes, I do, but I've heard they want to put on a musical, and I'm not good at singing.

Henry: Oh, OK, so no acting class for you. I think you should pick the band. You can draw in your free time. With the band you could find new friends and improve your guitar skills.

Paula: Thanks for your advice, Henry. I think I'll do exactly that.

Now listen again.

Text 3

What does Martha buy?

Girl: Mum asked me to go grocery shopping, but I need to finish my school project. Can you go for me, Martha?

Martha: I guess I can. What did Mum want you to buy?

Girl: Well, she wanted me to buy enough groceries for the whole week, and we're very short on things for breakfast.

Martha: So, what do you want for breakfast?

Girl: I guess some cereal as usual.

Martha: I don't want cereal every day. I think I'll buy some pancakes instead. Do we still have enough coffee and cream for Mum and Dad?

Girl: Yes, we do. But you'd better get some milk too. We've almost run out of it.

Martha: And what about some soft drinks?

Girl: No. Get some bottled water instead. That's better for us. OK, I'm all set to go. I'll be back soon.

Now listen again.

Text 4

What will Marc do next?

Marc: Hi, Mum.

Mum: Hi, Marc. What's up?

Marc: Oh, Mum, I'm so bored. Don't know what to do. This Covid thing sucks. You can't do anything.

Mum: I know what you mean, love. But we all have to go through this. What about reading a book? You got that new one last week?

Marc: Boring! Reading is so old school. I'd love to play football with my friends.

Mum: Of course, you would. What about some exercises via YouTube? There are so many videos.

Marc: Doesn't sound that bad, but on my own?

Mum: What about me motivating you from the sofa?

Marc: Please, Mum, you realise how strange that sounds? Oh, no. I have a video conference with my English class in 10 minutes.

Mum: Problem solved!

Now listen again.

Text 5

What present will Peter buy for Sally's birthday?

Peter: Hey, Anna. Sally's invited me to her birthday party next Saturday. Since you're her sister, I was wondering if you've any idea what I could bring as a present.

Anna: Oh, that's a tough question. Let me think. Her phone broke last week. I'm sure she would be happy to get a new one.

Peter: Well, that might be a bit too expensive for me. Is there something else she would like?

Anna: Well, I know that she plans to visit a festival this summer. She's still looking for a sleeping bag, and she needs a new backpack.

Peter: Oh, that sounds better. Maybe I could get a sleeping bag in her favorite color.

Anna: She likes pink. But I just remembered my parents said they want to buy her one, so maybe you better look for a pink backpack then.

Peter: Ah, OK, I'll do that. Thanks for your advice. I'll see you on Saturday at the party!

Now listen again.

Text 6

What pet will the family get?

Son: Hey, Dad. You remember you promised to get us a pet this summer? I would really like a dog.

Dad: Yes, I talked to your mother about that. We aren't sure what to get. There are a lot of responsibilities. You'll have to go for walks with the dog every day.

Son: Even if it rains?

Dad: Yes, even then. And your sister wants a rabbit to cuddle. Maybe that's the pet we should get.

Son: But, Dad, rabbits are so boring. They just sit in their cage all day long. I want a pet I can play with and take outside.

Dad: What about a cat then? You can play with it. You don't have to take it out every day and your sister can cuddle it. So that's a perfect compromise – and I always wanted a cat.

Son: OK, if you think so …

Now listen again.

Part 2

Now turn to part 2, questions 7 to 13. Listen to the following interview between Mrs. Moth and Fox Badger from the z-files YouTube channel. Mrs. Moth talks about a spooky experience in an old hotel in Scotland. For questions 7 to 13 tick the correct box A, B, or C. The first question is an example. You now have 30 seconds to look at part 2.
Now we are ready to start. Listen carefully. You will hear the recording twice.

Fox Badger: Welcome to the z-files, our great YouTube channel! Thank you for coming, Mrs. Moth. Can you share with our viewers the spooky experience you had in Edinburgh last year?

Mrs. Moth: It surely was a spooky situation. My husband and I went to Edinburgh for the first time. We were staying in an old house, you know, and had a ghost experience that really caused us a few shivers.

Fox Badger: What happened?

Mrs. Moth: We were in our hotel room, which was on a rather creaky corridor. It was a very old house in a long city street from the 1750s or something like that.

Fox Badger: And then …

Mrs. Moth: Well, we were just sitting on the sofa and watching TV with my husband on my left. Suddenly, everything went off, the lights, the TV, and then within a few seconds, it felt as if there was someone very close to me on the other side. I heard a sort of breathing, a kind of quiet and soft breathing.

Fox Badger: That sounds really spooky. How did you react?

Mrs. Moth: I mean, there couldn't have been anyone there because all there was next to me was an old wardrobe, you know? Actually, there was no room for another person to stand there. But the sound of breathing was very, very real. I couldn't believe this was really happening, and I thought somebody was making fun of me, so I asked my husband, "Do you hear what I hear"?

Fox Badger: And could he hear it as well? What did he say?

Mrs. Moth: He whispered, "Yes". So I asked quietly, "Do you see anything?" And he said he didn't, so he switched on the light, and the really weird thing was that the moment the light came on, the breathing stopped, and I could see a transparent figure just disappearing into the wardrobe.

Fox Badger: Really? Oh, that is spooky. What did you do next?

Mrs. Moth: I mean, I couldn't stay in that room a moment longer, so we went down to the reception and spoke to the manager. He smiled and told us that we were not the first people to see the ghost. It might have been the first owner of that house and our room was his bedroom. But he said not to be afraid because it was a friendly ghost. There wasn't another room available, so we had to go back to our room.

Fox Badger: And did you see the ghost again?

Mrs. Moth: No, we didn't. We actually slept very well that night. Maybe the ghost just wanted to check who was in his bedroom now …

Now listen again.

This is the end of part 2.

Part 3

Now turn to part 3, questions 14 to 21. Listen to this announcement for a talent show in Monmouth, a town in Wales. For questions 14 to 21 fill in the gaps to complete the notes. The first question is an example. You now have 30 seconds to look at part 3.
Now we are ready to start. Listen carefully. You will hear the recording twice.

Speaker: The popular student event called *Monmouth's Got Talent* is back this year and this time it's online. *Monmouth's Got Talent* is adapted from the popular BBC television show *Britain's Got Talent.* Every year, British people of any age can apply for the television contest with whatever talent they wish to present. *Monmouth's Got Talent* will give Monmouth students the chance to represent their school and demonstrate their skills, whether it's magic, singing or playing an instrument. This year, there are no limits. The students are not performing on an actual stage. They can be creative and show their talent in a video. Students can enter on their own or as a group. All three secondary schools in Monmouth can take part in the event. There will be no age limit, so students from years 5 to 10 are welcome to enter the fun contest. Apart from the fun factor, this is a charity event which wants to raise money for a good cause. This year the money that people donate will support the Trussell Trust, a network of food banks across the United Kingdom. The trust helps people in need with emergency food. Details of how you can give money will follow shortly on the school's websites and in a letter to parents. You want to know how you can enter? Simply think about what you're really good at and send your video to students@monmouth.co.uk. It shouldn't be longer than four minutes and it must reach us by 30 May. Please include your name and form so we can contact the finalists. The date for announcing the finalists is 6 June and the videos of the three winners will be featured on YouTube on 26 June. Get in touch with the organisers if you have any questions or need support. And last but not least, there's a £ 50 prize for the winning act, as well as two runner-up prizes of £ 25.

Now listen to part 3 again.

This is the end of part 3.

Part 4

Now turn to part 4, questions 22 to 28. You will hear an interview with Andy Keating, the guitar player of the band IST IST from Manchester. He talks about the effects COVID 19 has on the music industry in Greater Manchester.
For questions 22 to 28 decide whether each sentence is true or false. Put a tick in the correct box "true" or "false". The first question is an example.
You now have 30 seconds to look at part 4.
Now we are ready to start. Listen carefully. You will hear the recording twice.

Host: Welcome to our show today. With me is Andy Keating, the guitar player of the band IST IST. And we're talking about the effects of Covid 19 on the Manchester music industry. Andy, Covid has hit the music industry hard, especially in Manchester.

Andy Keating: Absolutely. Hundreds of gigs had to be cancelled. Concert halls have closed.

Host: What was it like for your band?

Andy Keating: For our band, the impact of the pandemic has been massive. We released our album *Architecture* in May 2020. We were about to start a tour. Quite a lot of tickets had been sold and then the gigs were cancelled, and we had to set new dates.

Host: How did that feel?

Andy Keating: We felt a kind of panic when we were stopped before it even began. We had the feeling this album was so good it would make it into the charts. But if you can't tour, the album won't sell.

Host: That's bad to hear, but I'm sure you are not the only band with this problem.

Andy Keating: Musicians need tours to reach out to the audience. You lose a lot of money if you don't sell tickets or CDs. That's why several musicians had a lot of problems and had to take on totally different jobs to earn money.

Host: It sounds like a disaster for the Manchester music scene.

Andy Keating: As hard as these times were, there are reasons to be positive about the near future. People are desperate to go out. The very moment nightclubs are allowed to open again people are going to go there.

Host: What do you think will change or will the concerts be the same as before?

Andy Keating: A lot of things will change. I think people will either need to show a vaccine passport on a phone or take a quick test on the door. And we're going to have to put hand sanitiser points everywhere. I also expect many places not to accept cash. I think the days of cash are perhaps finished.

Host: It seems like music will look different post-Covid. I hope that we can soon live in a Manchester again where there's amazing, exciting, creative and cultural things happening everywhere.

Andy Keating: I'm positive about it. It will take a while to start performing again when restrictions are lifted, but we're really looking forward to it and we hope we can start touring Great Britain after summer.

Host: We hope so, too. Thanks for the interview. Good luck for the future!

Now listen to part 4 again.

This is the end of the listening part. Good luck for the rest of your examination!

Bildnachweis
E-Kurs
2022-4 © Can Stock Photo / korvin79

G-Kurs
2022-30 © Dima Moro/shutterstock
2022-31 https://kurzelinks.de/y5p1
2022-33 Image Source/iStock

Abschlussarbeiten an der IGS in Niedersachsen
Englisch 2023

Um dir die Prüfung 2023 schnellstmöglich zur Verfügung stellen zu können, bringen wir sie in digitaler Form heraus.

Sobald die Original-Prüfungsaufgaben 2023 freigegeben sind, können sie als PDF auf der Plattform *MyStark* heruntergeladen werden (Zugangscode vgl. Umschlaginnenseite).

Aktuelle Prüfung

www.stark-verlag.de/mystark